# The Great Spell

The words of the enchantment hissed and mumbled on Ged's lips, and then he cried aloud . . . "Elfarran!" Again he cried the name. And the third time . . .

The shapeless mass of darkness split apart. It sundered, and a pale spindle of light gleamed between his open arms. In the oval of light there moved a human shape: a tall woman . . . beautiful, and sorrowful, and full of fear.

Only for a moment did the spirit glimmer there. Then the oval grew bright . . . and through it blazed a terrible brightness . . . and through that breach clambered something like a clot of black shadow, quick and hideous, and it leaped straight out at Ged's face.

# A WIZARD OF EARTHSEA
## by Ursula K. Le Guin

*Illustrated by Ruth Robbins*

BANTAM BOOKS
TORONTO · NEW YORK · LONDON · SYDNEY

*This low-priced Bantam Book
has been completely reset in a type face
designed for easy reading, and was printed
from new plates. It contains the complete
text of the original hard-cover edition.*
NOT ONE WORD HAS BEEN OMITTED.

A WIZARD OF EARTHSEA

*A Bantam Book / published by arrangement with
Parnassus Press*

**PRINTING HISTORY**

*Parnassus Press edition published November 1968
2nd printing .. December 1969
Bantam edition / August 1975
2nd printing
3rd printing
4th printing
5th printing*

*Bantam Books are published by Bantam Books, Inc. Its trade-
mark, consisting of the words "Bantam Books" and the por-
trayal of a bantam, is registered in the United States Patent
Office and in other countries. Marca Registrada. Bantam
Books, Inc., 666 Fifth Avenue, New York, New York 10019.*

PRINTED IN THE UNITED STATES OF AMERICA

*To my brothers*
*Clifton, Ted, Karl*

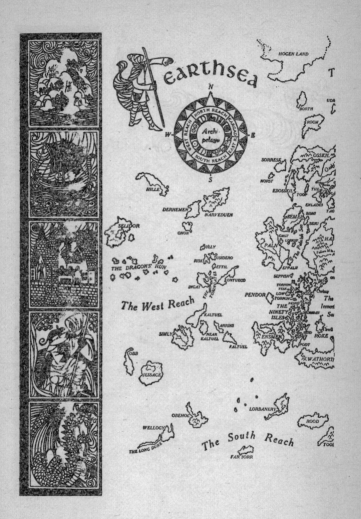

**EARTHSEA**

HOGEN LAND

NORTH REACH

Arch-
pelago

WEST REACH                    EAST REACH

SOUTH REACH

BORTH                    UDA

ROGM

SORRESK                    OSSKIL

NORST                    THED

HILLE                    EDOSSIL    TOOK    FAG

ENLADES
BIMBI    BERU

DERHEMEN                    SEMEL

NARVEDUEN                    CALIT    LORBO    HA...

GONT                    PALN

SELIDOR                    Falkern N.b.
                          Felkway

JULLY                    EPPALN

RISK    USIDERO                    SEPPISH

THE DRAGONS' RUN    GETTIL    TORNING
                    INGAT            FEXT
                    ONTUEGO    PENDOR    LOW    The
                    THE TORIKLES    TORNING    Inmost
                    TORNING    Se...

**The West Reach**    THE
                    NINETY
                    ISLES

                    KALTUEL    ...ORDE

SIMLY    ARRUNS    ENSMER    ROKE
        NEAR
        KALTUEL    FALTUEL    POOT

OBB                    KWATHORT

JESSAGE

                    LORBANERY

OBEHOL                    ROOD

WELLOGY

THE LONG DUNE    **The South Reach**    TOO...

FAR SORR

THE WHALE ISLES

he North Reach

N. ENWAS
BERESWEK
S. ENWAS

KOMOKOME
SORT

CHEMISH

THE ALLERNOTS

FENUNS

THE TEETH
THE ANDRADES
N. TEETH
The Jaws
S. TEETH
ANDRAD
KORANDRAD

ORANEA
EBEA

CONTE
KAMEBER
East Port
Goat Port
PERREGAL

The Kargad Lands

HUR-
AT-HUR

BARNISK

Gontish
Sea

SPEVY

KAREGO-AT
ATUAN

ATNINI

WOR

ESKEL
O'TORIKLES

TORHEVEN

THEN

WAY
IOTRAD

THE HANDS

VEMISH
SATTINS
YOR

Harbour
Great Port

TELKSAY

WAYMARSH

VENWAY
IFFISH
Ismay
TOK

SNEG

FAR TOLY

ILIEN
VEMI
LENG

PERILANE
OUTER
SHRAH

KOPPISH

IHKMER

HOLP

RAMERY

The Ninety Isles

TORK

KORP
KOPP
APSU

SODERS
CALE

PELIMER

GOSK

SOWL
NAMIEN
HOLAMENY

The East Reach

KORNAY

MISE
SETO
DUNNEL

ASTOWELL

WASNY

GREAT SOUTH SHOALS

THE ISLE
OF THE EAR

25 50   100   150   200   300

A Scale of Miles

Only in silence the word,
only in dark the light,
only in dying life:
bright the hawk's flight
on the empty sky.
　　　　　*—The Creation of Éa*

# 1 Warriors in the Mist

The island of Gont, a single mountain that lifts its peak a mile above the storm-racked Northeast Sea, is a land famous for wizards. From the towns in its high valleys and the ports on its dark narrow bays many a Gontishman has gone forth to serve the Lords of the Archipelago in their cities as wizard or mage, or, looking for adventure, to wander working magic from isle to isle of all Earthsea. Of these some say the greatest, and surely the greatest voyager, was the man called Sparrowhawk, who in his day became both dragonlord and Archmage. His life is told of in the *Deed of Ged* and in many songs, but this is a tale of the time before his fame, before the songs were made.

He was born in a lonely village called Ten Alders, high on the mountain at the head of the Northward Vale. Below the village the pastures and plowlands of the Vale slope downward level below level towards the sea, and other towns lie on the bends of the River Ar; above the village only forest rises ridge behind

1

ridge to the stone and snow of the heights.

The name he bore as a child, Duny, was given him
by his mother, and that and his life were all she
could give him, for she died before he was a year old.
His father, the bronze-smith of the village, was a grim
unspeaking man, and since Duny's six brothers were
older than he by many years and went one by one
from home to farm the land or sail the sea or work as
smith in other towns of the Northward Vale, there
was no one to bring the child up in tenderness. He
grew wild, a thriving weed, a tall, quick boy, loud
and proud and full of temper. With the few other
children of the village he herded goats on the steep
meadows above the river-springs; and when he was
strong enough to push and pull the long bellows-
sleeves, his father made him work as smith's boy, at a
high cost in blows and whippings. There was not
much work to be got out of Duny. He was always off
and away; roaming deep in the forest, swimming in
the pools of the River Ar that like all Gontish rivers
runs very quick and cold, or climbing by cliff and
scarp to the heights above the forest, from which he
could see the sea, that broad northern ocean where,
past Perregal, no islands are.

A sister of his dead mother lived in the village. She
had done what was needful for him as a baby, but
she had business of her own and once he could look
after himself at all she paid no more heed to him. But
one day when the boy was seven years old, untaught
and knowing nothing of the arts and powers that are
in the world, he heard his aunt crying out words to a
goat which had jumped up onto the thatch of a hut
and would not come down: but it came jumping
when she cried a certain rhyme to it. Next day herd-
ing the longhaired goats on the meadows of High
Fall, Duny shouted to them the words he had heard,
not knowing their use or meaning or what kind of
words they were:

*Noth hierth malk man*
*hiolk han merth han!*

He yelled the rhyme aloud, and the goats came to
him. They came very quickly, all of them together,
not making any sound. They looked at him out of the
dark slot in their yellow eyes.

Duny laughed and shouted it out again, the rhyme
that gave him power over the goats. They came
closer, crowding and pushing round him. All at once
he felt afraid of their thick, ridged horns and their
strange eyes and their strange silence. He tried to get
free of them and to run away. The goats ran with
him keeping in a knot around him, and so they came
charging down into the village at last, all the goats
going huddled together as if a rope were pulled tight
round them, and the boy in the midst of them weeping and bellowing. Villagers ran from their houses to
swear at the goats and laugh at the boy. Among them
came the boy's aunt, who did not laugh. She said a
word to the goats, and the beasts began to bleat and
browse and wander, freed from the spell.

"Come with me," she said to Duny.

She took him into her hut where she lived alone.
She let no child enter there usually, and the children
feared the place. It was low and dusky, windowless,
fragrant with herbs that hung drying from the cross-
pole of the roof, mint and moly and thyme, yarrow
and rushwash and paramal, kingsfoil, clovenfoot,
tansy and bay. There his aunt sat crosslegged by the
firepit, and looking sidelong at the boy through the
tangles of her black hair she asked him what he had
said to the goats, and if he knew what the rhyme
was. When she found that he knew nothing, and yet
had spellbound the goats to come to him and follow
him, then she saw that he must have in him the mak-
ings of power.

As her sister's son he had been nothing to her, but
now she looked at him with a new eye. She praised

him, and told him she might teach him rhymes he would like better, such as the word that makes a snail look out of its shell, or the name that calls a falcon down from the sky.

"Aye, teach me that name!" he said, being clear over the fright the goats had given him, and puffed up with her praise of his cleverness.

The witch said to him, "You will not ever tell that word to the other children, if I teach it to you."

"I promise."

She smiled at his ready ignorance. "Well and good. But I will bind your promise. Your tongue will be stilled until I choose to unbind it, and even then, though you can speak, you will not be able to speak the word I teach you where another person can hear it. We must keep the secrets of our craft."

"Good," said the boy, for he had no wish to tell the secret to his playmates, liking to know and do what they knew not and could not.

He sat still while his aunt bound back her un-combed hair, and knotted the belt of her dress, and again sat cross-legged throwing handfuls of leaves into the firepit, so that a smoke spread and filled the darkness of the hut. She began to sing. Her voice changed sometimes to low or high as if another voice sang through her, and the singing went on and on until the boy did not know if he waked or slept, and all the while the witch's old black dog that never barked sat by him with eyes red from the smoke. Then the witch spoke to Duny in a tongue he did not understand, and made him say with her certain rhymes and words until the enchantment came on him and held him still.

"Speak!" she said to test the spell.

The boy could not speak, but he laughed.

Then his aunt was a little afraid of his strength, for this was as strong a spell as she knew how to weave: she had tried not only to gain control of his speech and silence, but to bind him at the same time to her service in the craft of sorcery. Yet even as the spell bound him, he had laughed. She said nothing. She threw clear water on the fire till the smoke cleared away, and gave the boy water to drink, and when the air was clear and he could speak again she taught him the true name of the falcon, to which the falcon must come.

This was Duny's first step on the way he was to follow all his life, the way of magery, the way that led him at last to hunt a shadow over land and sea to the lightless coasts of death's kingdom. But in those first steps along the way, it seemed a broad, bright road.

When he found that the wild falcons stooped down to him from the wind when he summoned them by name, lighting with a thunder of wings on his wrist like the hunting-birds of a prince, then he hungered to know more such names and came to his aunt begging to learn the name of the sparrowhawk and the osprey and the eagle. To earn the words of power he did all the witch asked of him and learned of her all she taught, though not all of it was pleasant to do or know. There is a saying on Gont, *Weak as woman's magic,* and there is another saying, *Wicked as woman's magic.* Now the witch of Ten Alders was no black sorceress, nor did she ever meddle with the high arts or traffic with Old Powers; but being an ignorant woman among ignorant folk, she often used her crafts to foolish and dubious ends. She knew nothing of the Balance and the Pattern which the true wizard knows and serves, and which keep him from using his spells unless real need demands. She had a spell for every circumstance, and was forever weaving charms. Much of her lore was mere rubbish and humbug, nor did she know the true spells from the false. She knew many curses, and was better at causing sickness, perhaps, than at curing it. Like any village witch she could brew up a love-potion, but there were other, uglier brews she made to serve men's jealousy and hate. Such practices, however, she kept from her young prentice, and as far as she was able she taught him honest craft.

At first all his pleasure in the art-magic was, child-like, the power it gave him over bird and beast, and the knowledge of these. And indeed that pleasure stayed with him all his life. Seeing him in the high pastures often with a bird of prey about him, the other children called him Sparrowhawk, and so he came by the name that he kept in later life as his use-name, when his true-name was not known.

As the witch kept talking of the glory and the riches and the great power over men that a sorcerer could gain, he set himself to learn more useful lore. He was very quick at it. The witch praised him and the children of the village began to fear him, and he himself was sure that very soon he would become great among men. So he went on from word to word and from spell to spell with the witch till he was twelve years old and had learned from her a great part of what she knew: not much, but enough for the witchwife of a small village, and more than enough for a boy of twelve. She had taught him all her lore in herbals and healing, and all she knew of the crafts of finding, binding, mending, unsealing and revealing. What she knew of chanters' tales and the great Deeds she had sung him, and all the words of the True Speech that she had learned from the sorcerer that taught her, she taught again to Duny. And from weatherworkers and wandering jugglers who went from town to town of the Northward Vale and the East Forest he had learned various tricks and pleas-antries, spells of Illusion. It was with one of these light spells that he first proved the great power that was in him.

In those days the Kargad Empire was strong. Those are four great lands that lie between the Northern and the Eastern Reaches: Karego-At, Atuan, Hur-at-Hur, Atnini. The tongue they speak there is not like any spoken in the Archipelago or the other Reaches, and they are a savage people, white-skinned, yellow-haired, and fierce, liking the sight of blood and the smell of burning towns. Last year they had attacked the Torikles and the strong island Torheven, raiding in great force in fleets of red-sailed ships. News of this came north to Gont, but the Lords of Gont were busy with their piracy and paid small heed to the woes of other lands. Then Spevy fell to the Kargs and was looted and laid waste, its people taken as slaves, so that even now it is an isle of ruins. In lust of conquest the Kargs sailed next to Gont, coming in a host, thirty great longships, to East Port. They fought through that town, took it, burned it; leaving their ships under guard at the mouth of the River Ar they went up the Vale wrecking and looting, slaughtering cattle and men. As they went they split to bands, and each of these bands plundered where it chose. Fugitives brought warning to the villages of the heights. Soon the people of Ten Alders saw smoke darken the eastern sky, and that night those who climbed the High Fall looked down on the Vale all hazed and red-streaked with fires where fields ready for harvest had been set ablaze, and orchards burned, the fruit roasting on the blazing boughs, and barns and farmhouses smouldered in ruin.

Some of the villagers fled up the ravines and hid in the forest, and some made ready to fight for their lives, and some did neither but stood about lamenting. The witch was one who fled, hiding alone in a cave up on the Kapperding Scarp and sealing the cave-mouth with spells. Duny's father the bronze-smith was one who stayed, for he would not leave his smelting-pit and forge where he had worked for fifty years. All that night he labored beating up what ready metal he had there into spearpoints, and others worked with him binding these to the handles of hoes and rakes, there being no time to make sockets and shaft them properly. There had been no weapons in

the village but hunting bows and short knives, for the
mountain folk of Gont are not warlike; it is not warriors they are famous for, but goat-thieves, sea-pi-
rates, and wizards.

With sunrise came a thick white fog, as on many
autumn mornings in the heights of the island. Among
their huts and houses down the straggling street of
Ten Alders the villagers stood waiting with their hunting bows and new-forged spears, not knowing whether the Kargs might be far off or very near, all silent,
all peering into the fog that hid shapes and distances
and dangers from their eyes.

With them was Duny. He had worked all night at
the forge-bellows, pushing and pulling the two long
sleeves of goathide that fed the fire with a blast of
air. Now his arms so ached and trembled from that
work that he could not hold out the spear he had
chosen. He did not see how he could fight or be of
any good to himself or the villagers. It rankled at his
heart that he should die, spitted on a Kargish lance,
while still a boy: that he should go into the dark land
without ever having known his own name, his true
name as a man. He looked down at his thin arms, wet
with cold fog-dew, and raged at his weakness, for he
knew his strength. There was power in him, if he
knew how to use it, and he sought among all the
spells he knew for some device that might give him
and his companions an advantage, or at least a
chance. But need alone is not enough to set power
free: there must be knowledge.

The fog was thinning now under the heat of the
sun that shone bare above on the peak in a bright
sky. As the mists moved and parted in great drifts
and smoky wisps, the villagers saw a band of warriors
coming up the mountain. They were armored with
bronze helmets and greaves and breastplates of heavy
leather and shields of wood and bronze, and armed
with swords and the long Kargish lance. Winding up
along the steep bank of the Ar they came in a

plumed, clanking, straggling line, near enough already that their white faces could be seen, and the words of their jargon heard as they shouted to one another. In this band of the invading horde there were about a hundred men, which is not many; but in the village were only eighteen men and boys.

Now need called knowledge out: Duny, seeing the fog blow and thin across the path before the Kargs, saw a spell that might avail him. An old weather-worker of the Vale, seeking to win the boy as prentice, had taught him several charms. One of these tricks was called fogweaving, a binding-spell that gathers the mists together for a while in one place; with it one skilled in illusion can shape the mist into fair ghostly seemings, which last a little and fade away. The boy had no such skill, but his intent was different, and he had the strength to turn the spell to his own ends. Rapidly and aloud he named the places and the boundaries of the village, and then spoke the fogweaving charm, but in among its words he enlaced the words of a spell of concealment, and last he cried the word that set the magic going.

Even as he did so his father coming up behind him struck him hard on the side of the head, knocking him right down. "Be still, fool! keep your blattering mouth shut, and hide if you can't fight!"

Duny got to his feet. He could hear the Kargs now at the end of the village, as near as the great yew-tree by the tanner's yard. Their voices were clear, and the clink and creak of their harness and arms, but they could not be seen. The fog had closed and thickened all over the village, greying the light, blurring the world till a man could hardly see his own hands before him.

"I've hidden us all," Duny said, sullenly, for his head hurt from his father's blow, and the working of the doubled incantation had drained his strength. "I'll keep up this fog as long as I can. Get the others to lead them up to High Fall."

The smith stared at his son who stood wraithlike in that weird, dank mist. It took him a minute to see Duny's meaning, but when he did he ran at once, noiselessly, knowing every fence and corner of the village, to find the others and tell them what to do. Now through the grey fog bloomed a blur of red, as the Kargs set fire to the thatch of a house. Still they did not come up into the village, but waited at the lower end till the mist should lift and lay bare their loot and prey.

The tanner, whose house it was that burned, sent a couple of boys skipping right under the Kargs' noses, taunting and yelling and vanishing again like smoke into smoke. Meantime the older men, creeping behind fences and running from house to house, came close on the other side and sent a volley of arrows and spears at the warriors, who stood all in a bunch. One Karg fell writhing with a spear, still warm from its forging, right through his body. Others were arrow-bitten, and all enraged. They charged forward then to hew down their puny attackers, but they found only the fog about them, full of voices. They followed the voices, stabbing ahead into the mist with their great, plumed, bloodstained lances. Up the length of the street they came shouting, and never knew they had run right through the village, as the empty huts and houses loomed and disappeared again in the writhing grey fog. The villagers ran scattering, most of them keeping well ahead since they knew the ground; but some, boys or old men, were slow. The Kargs stumbling on them drove their lances or hacked with their swords, yelling their war-cry, the names of the White Godbrothers of Atuan:

"Wuluah! Atwah!"

Some of the band stopped when they felt the land grow rough underfoot, but others pressed right on, seeking the phantom village, following dim wavering shapes that fled just out of reach before them. All the mist had come alive with these fleeting forms,

dodging, flickering, fading on every side. One group
of the Kargs chased the wraiths straight to the High
Fall, the cliff's edge above the springs of Ar, and the
shapes they pursued ran out onto the air and there
vanished in a thinning of the mist, while the pursuers
fell screaming through fog and sudden sunlight a
hundred feet sheer to the shallow pools among the
rocks. And those that came behind and did not fall
stood at the cliff's edge, listening.

Now dread came into the Kargs' hearts and they
began to seek one another, not the villagers, in the
uncanny mist. They gathered on the hillside, and yet
always there were wraiths and ghost-shapes among
them, and other shapes that ran and stabbed from behind with spear or knife and vanished again. The
Kargs began to run, all of them, downhill, stumbling,
silent, until all at once they ran out from the grey
blind mist and saw the river and the ravines below
the village all bare and bright in morning sunlight.
Then they stopped, gathering together, and looked
back. A wall of wavering, writhing grey lay blank
across the path, hiding all that lay behind it. Out
from it burst two or three stragglers, lunging and
stumbling along, their long lances rocking on their
shoulders. Not one Karg looked back more than that
once. All went down, in haste, away from the enchanted place.

Farther down the Northward Vale those warriors
got their fill of fighting. The towns of the East Forest,
from Ovark to the coast, had gathered their men and
sent them against the invaders of Gont. Band after
band they came down from the hills, and that day
and the next the Kargs were harried back down to
the beaches above East Port, where they found their
ships burnt; so they fought with their backs to the sea
till every man of them was killed, and the sands of
Armouth were brown with blood until the tide came
in.

But on that morning in Ten Alders village and up

on the High Fall, the dank grey fog had clung a
while, and then suddenly it blew and drifted and
melted away. This man and that stood up in the
windy brightness of the morning, and looked about
him wondering. Here lay a dead Karg with yellow
hair long, loose, and bloody; there lay the village tanner, killed in battle like a king.

Down in the village the house that had been set
afire still blazed. They ran to put the fire out, since
their battle had been won. In the street, near the
great yew, they found Duny the bronze-smith's son
standing by himself, bearing no hurt, but speechless
and stupid like one stunned. They were well aware of
what he had done, and they led him into his father's
house and went calling for the witch to come down
out of her cave and heal the lad who had saved their
lives and their property, all but four who were killed
by the Kargs, and the one house that was burnt.

No weapon-hurt had come to the boy, but he
would not speak nor eat nor sleep; he seemed not to
hear what was said to him, not to see those who came
to see him. There was none in those parts wizard
enough to cure what ailed him. His aunt said, "He
has overspent his power," but she had no art to help
him.

While he lay thus dark and dumb, the story of the
lad who wove the fog and scared off Kargish swords-
men with a mess of shadows was told all down the
Northward Vale, and in the East Forest, and high on
the mountain and over the mountain even in the
Great Port of Gont. So it happened that on the fifth
day after the slaughter at Armouth a stranger came
into Ten Alders village, a man neither young nor old,
who came cloaked and bareheaded, lightly carrying a
great staff of oak that was as tall as himself. He did
not come up the course of the Ar like most people,
but down, out of the forests of the higher mountain-
side. The village goodwives saw well that he was a
wizard, and when he told them that he was a healall,

they brought him straight to the smith's house. Sending away all but the boy's father and aunt the stranger stooped above the cot where Duny lay staring into the dark, and did no more than lay his hand on the boy's forehead and touch his lips once.

Duny sat up slowly looking about him. In a little while he spoke, and strength and hunger began to come back into him. They gave him a little to drink and eat, and he lay back again, always watching the stranger with dark wondering eyes.

The bronze-smith said to that stranger, "You are no common man."

"Nor will this boy be a common man," the other answered. "The tale of his deed with the fog has come to Re Albi, which is my home. I have come here to give him his name, if as they say he has not yet made his passage into manhood."

The witch whispered to the smith, "Brother, this must surely be the Mage of Re Albi, Ogion the Silent, that one who tamed the earthquake—"

"Sir," said the bronze-smith who would not let a great name daunt him, "my son will be thirteen this month coming, but we thought to hold his Passage at the feast of Sunreturn this winter."

"Let him be named as soon as may be," said the mage, "for he needs his name. I have other business now, but I will come back here for the day you choose. If you see fit I will take him with me when I go thereafter. And if he prove apt I will keep him as prentice, or see to it that he is schooled as fits his gifts. For to keep dark the mind of the mageborn, that is a dangerous thing."

Very gently Ogion spoke, but with certainty, and even the hardheaded smith assented to all he said.

On the day the boy was thirteen years old, a day in the early splendor of autumn while still the bright leaves are on the trees, Ogion returned to the village from his rovings over Gont Mountain, and the ceremony of Passage was held. The witch took from the boy his name Duny, the name his mother had given him as a baby. Nameless and naked he walked into the cold springs of the Ar where it rises among rocks under the high cliffs. As he entered the water clouds crossed the sun's face and great shadows slid and mingled over the water of the pool about him. He crossed to the far bank, shuddering with cold but walking slow and erect as he should through that icy, living water. As he came to the bank Ogion, waiting, reached out his hand and clasping the boy's arm whispered to him his true name: Ged.

Thus was he given his name by one very wise in the uses of power.

The feasting was far from over, and all the villagers were making merry with plenty to eat and beer to drink and a chanter from down the Vale singing the *Deed of the Dragonlords,* when the mage spoke in his quiet voice to Ged: "Come, lad. Bid your people farewell and leave them feasting."

Ged fetched what he had to carry, which was the good bronze knife his father had forged him, and a leather coat the tanner's widow had cut down to his size, and an alder-stick his aunt had becharmed for him: that was all he owned besides his shirt and breeches. He said farewell to them, all the people he knew in all the world, and looked about once at the village that straggled and huddled there under the cliffs, over the river-springs. Then he set off with his new master through the steep slanting forests of the mountain isle, through the leaves and shadows of bright autumn.

## 2 The Shadow

Ged had thought that as the prentice of a great mage he would enter at once into the mystery and mastery of power. He would understand the language of the beasts and the speech of the leaves of the forest, he thought, and sway the winds with his word, and learn to change himself into any shape he wished. Maybe he and his master would run together as stags, or fly to Re Albi over the mountain on the wings of eagles.

But it was not so at all. They wandered, first down into the Vale and then gradually south and westward around the mountain, given lodging in little villages or spending the night out in the wilderness, like poor journeyman-sorcerers, or tinkers, or beggars. They entered no mysterious domain. Nothing happened. The mage's oaken staff that Ged had watched at first with eager dread was nothing but a stout staff to walk with. Three days went by and four days went by and still Ogion had not spoken a single charm in Ged's hearing, and had not taught him a single name or rune or spell.

Though a very silent man he was so mild and calm that Ged soon lost his awe of him, and in a day or two more he was bold enough to ask his master, "When will my apprenticeship begin, Sir?"

"It has begun," said Ogion.

There was a silence, as if Ged was keeping back something he had to say. Then he said it: "But I haven't learned anything yet!"

"Because you haven't found out what I am teaching," replied the mage, going on at his steady, long-legged pace along their road, which was the high pass between Ovark and Wiss. He was a dark man, like most Gontishmen, dark copper-brown; grey-haired, lean and tough as a hound, tireless. He spoke seldom, ate little, slept less. His eyes and ears were very keen, and often there was a listening look on his face.

Ged did not answer him. It is not always easy to answer a mage.

"You want to work spells," Ogion said presently, striding along. "You've drawn too much water from that well. Wait. Manhood is patience. Mastery is nine times patience. What is that herb by the path?"

"Strawflower."

"And that?"

"I don't know."

"Fourfoil, they call it." Ogion had halted, the coppershod foot of his staff near the little weed, so Ged looked closely at the plant, and plucked a dry seedpod from it, and finally asked, since Ogion said nothing more, "What is its use, Master?"

"None I know of."

Ged kept the seedpod a while as they went on, then tossed it away.

"When you know the fourfoil in all its seasons root and leaf and flower, by sight and scent and seed, then you may learn its true name, knowing its being: which is more than its use. What, after all, is the use of you? or of myself? Is Gont Mountain useful, or the

Open Sea?" Ogion went on a halfmile or so, and said at last, "To hear, one must be silent."

The boy frowned. He did not like to be made to feel a fool. He kept back his resentment and impatience, and tried to be obedient, so that Ogion would consent at last to teach him something. For he hungered to learn, to gain power. It began to seem to him, though, that he could have learned more walking with any herb-gatherer or village sorcerer, and as they went round the mountain westward into the lonely forests past Wiss he wondered more and more what was the greatness and the magic of this great Mage Ogion. For when it rained Ogion would not even say the spell that every weatherworker knows, to send the storm aside. In a land where sorcerers come thick, like Gont or the Enlades, you may see a raincloud blundering slowly from side to side and place to place as one spell shunts it on to the next, till at last it is buffeted out over the sea where it can rain in peace. But Ogion let the rain fall where it would. He found a thick fir-tree and lay down beneath it. Ged crouched among the dripping bushes wet and sullen, and wondered what was the good of having power if you were too wise to use it, and wished he had gone as prentice to that old weatherworker of the Vale, where at least he would have slept dry. He did not speak any of his thoughts aloud. He said not a word. His master smiled, and fell asleep in the rain.

Along towards Sunreturn when the first heavy snows began to fall in the heights of Gont they came to Re Albi, Ogion's home. It is a town on the edge of the high rocks of Overfell, and its name means Falcon's Nest. From it one can see far below the deep harbor and the towers of the Port of Gont, and the ships that go in and out the gate of the bay between the Armed Cliffs, and far to the west across the sea one may make out the blue hills of Oranéa, eastern-most of the Inward Isles.

The mage's house, though large and soundly built

of timber, with hearth and chimney rather than a fire-pit, was like the huts of Ten Alders village: all one room, with a goatshed built onto one side. There was a kind of alcove in the west wall of the room, where Ged slept. Over his pallet was a window that looked out on the sea, but most often the shutters must be closed against the great winds that blew all winter from the west and north. In the dark warmth of that house Ged spent the winter, hearing the rush of rain and wind outside or the silence of snowfall, learning to write and read the Six Hundred Runes of Hardic. Very glad he was to learn this lore, for without it no mere rote-learning of charms and spells will give a man true mastery. The Hardic tongue of the Archipelago, though it has no more magic power in it than any other tongue of men, has its roots in the Old Speech, that language in which things are named with their true names: and the way to the understanding of this speech starts with the Runes that were written when the islands of the world first were raised up from the sea.

Still no marvels and enchantments occurred. All winter there was nothing but the heavy pages of the Runebook turning, and the rain and the snow falling; and Ogion would come in from roaming the icy forests or from looking after his goats, and stamp the snow off his boots, and sit down in silence by the fire. And the mage's long, listening silence would fill the room, and fill Ged's mind, until sometimes it seemed he had forgotten what words sounded like: and when Ogion spoke at last it was as if he had, just then and for the first time, invented speech. Yet the words he spoke were no great matters but had to do only with simple things, bread and water and weather and sleep.

As the spring came on, quick and bright, Ogion often sent Ged forth to gather herbs on the meadows above Re Albi, and told him to take as long as he liked about it, giving him freedom to spend all day

wandering by rainfilled streams and through the
woods and over wet green fields in the sun. Ged went
with delight each time, and stayed out till night; but
he did not entirely forget the herbs. He kept an eye
out for them, while he climbed and roamed and
waded and explored, and always brought some home.
He came on a meadow between two streams where
the flower called white hallows grew thick, and as
these blossoms are rare and prized by healers, he
came back again next day. Someone else was there
before him, a girl, whom he knew by sight as the
daughter of the old Lord of Re Albi. He would not
have spoken to her, but she came to him and greeted
him pleasantly: "I know you, you are the Sparrowhawk, our mage's adept. I wish you would tell me
about sorcery!"

He looked down at the white flowers that brushed
against her white skirt, and at first he was shy and
glum and hardly answered. But she went on talking,
in an open, careless, wilful way that little by little
set him at ease. She was a tall girl of about his own
age, very sallow, almost white-skinned; her mother,
they said in the village, was from Osskil or some such
foreign land. Her hair fell long and straight like a fall
of black water. Ged thought her very ugly, but he
had a desire to please her, to win her admiration, that
grew on him as they talked. She made him tell all the
story of his tricks with the mist that had defeated the
Kargish warriors, and she listened as if she wondered
and admired, but she spoke no praise. And soon she
was off on another tack: "Can you call the birds and
beasts to you?" she asked.

"I can," said Ged.

He knew there was a falcon's nest in the cliffs
above the meadow, and he summoned the bird by its
name. It came, but it would not light on his wrist,
being put off no doubt by the girl's presence. It
screamed and struck the air with broad barred wings,
and rose up on the wind.

"What do you call that kind of charm, that made the falcon come?"

"A spell of Summoning."

"Can you call the spirits of the dead to come to you, too?"

He thought she was mocking him with this question, because the falcon had not fully obeyed his summons. He would not let her mock him. "I might if I chose," he said in a calm voice.

"Is it not very difficult, very dangerous, to summon a spirit?"

"Difficult, yes. Dangerous?" He shrugged.

This time he was almost certain there was admiration in her eyes.

"Can you make a love-charm?"

"That is no mastery."

"True," says she, "any village witch can do it. Can you do Changing spells? Can you change your own shape, as wizards do, they say?"

Again he was not quite sure that she did not ask the question mockingly, and so again he replied, "I might if I chose."

She began to beg him to transform himself into anything he wished—a hawk, a bull, a fire, a tree. He put her off with short secretive words such as his master used, but he did not know how to refuse flatly when she coaxed him; and besides he did not know whether he himself believed his boast, or not. He left her, saying that his master the mage expected him at home, and he did not come back to the meadow the next day. But the day after he came again, saying to himself that he should gather more of the flowers while they bloomed. She was there, and together they waded barefoot in the boggy grass, pulling the heavy white hallow-blooms. The sun of spring shone, and she talked with him as merrily as any goatherd lass of his own village. She asked him again about sorcery, and listened wide-eyed to all he told her, so that he fell to boasting again. Then she asked him if he

would not work a Changing spell, and when he put
her off, she looked at him, putting back the black hair
from her face, and said, "Are you afraid to do it?"

"No, I am not afraid."

She smiled a little disdainfully and said, "Maybe
you are too young."

That he would not endure. He did not say much,
but he resolved that he would prove himself to her.
He told her to come again to the meadow tomorrow,
if she liked, and so took leave of her, and came back
to the house while his master was still out. He went
straight to the shelf and took down the two Lore-
Books, which Ogion had never yet opened in his
presence.

He looked for a spell of self-transformation, but
being slow to read the runes yet and understanding
little of what he read, he could not find what he
sought. These books were very ancient, Ogion having
them from his own master Heleth Farseer, and
Heleth from his master the Mage of Perregal, and so
back into the times of myth. Small and strange was
the writing, overwritten and interlined by many
hands, and all those hands were dust now. Yet here
and there Ged understood something of what he tried
to read, and with the girl's questions and her mockery
always in his mind, he stopped on a page that bore a
spell of summoning up the spirits of the dead.

As he read it, puzzling out the runes and symbols
one by one, a horror came over him. His eyes were
fixed, and he could not lift them till he had finished
reading all the spell.

Then raising his head he saw it was dark in the
house. He had been reading without any light, in the
darkness. He could not now make out the runes when
he looked down at the book. Yet the horror grew in
him, seeming to hold him bound in his chair. He was
cold. Looking over his shoulder he saw that something was crouching beside the closed door, a shapeless clot of shadow darker than the darkness. It

seemed to reach out towards him, and to whisper, and to call to him in a whisper: but he could not understand the words.

The door was flung wide. A man entered with a white light flaming about him, a great bright figure who spoke aloud, fiercely and suddenly. The darkness and the whispering ceased and were dispelled.

The horror went out of Ged, but still he was mortally afraid, for it was Ogion the Mage who stood there in the doorway with a brightness all about him, and the oaken staff in his hand burned with a white radiance.

Saying no word the mage came past Ged, and lighted the lamp, and put the books away on their shelf. Then he turned to the boy and said, "You will never work that spell but in peril of your power and your life. Was it for that spell you opened the books?"

"No, Master," the boy murmured, and shamefully he told Ogion what he had sought, and why.

"You do not remember what I told you, that that girl's mother, the Lord's wife, is an enchantress?"

Indeed Ogion had once said this, but Ged had not paid much attention, though he knew by now that Ogion never told him anything that he had not good reason to tell him.

"The girl herself is half a witch already. It may be the mother who sent the girl to talk to you. It may be she who opened the book to the page you read. The powers she serves are not the powers I serve: I do not know her will, but I know she does not will me well. Ged, listen to me now. Have you never thought how danger must surround power as shadow does light? This sorcery is not a game we play for pleasure or for praise. Think of this: that every word, every act of our Art is said and is done either for good, or for evil. Before you speak or do you must know the price that is to pay!"

Driven by his shame Ged cried, "How am I to know

these things, when you teach me nothing? Since I
lived with you I have done nothing, seen nothing—"

"Now you have seen something," said the mage.
"By the door, in the darkness, when I came in."

Ged was silent.

Ogion knelt down and built the fire on the hearth
and lit it, for the house was cold. Then still kneeling
he said in his quiet voice, "Ged, my young falcon,
you are not bound to me or to my service. You did
not come to me, but I to you. You are very young to
make this choice, but I cannot make it for you. If you
wish, I will send you to Roke Island, where all high
arts are taught. Any craft you undertake to learn
you will learn, for your power is great. Greater even
than your pride, I hope. I would keep you here with
me, for what I have is what you lack, but I will not
keep you against your will. Now choose between Re
Albi and Roke."

Ged stood dumb, his heart bewildered. He had
come to love this man Ogion who had healed him
with a touch, and who had no anger: he loved him,
and had not known it until now. He looked at the
oaken staff leaning in the chimney-corner, remembering the radiance of it that had burned out evil from
the dark, and he yearned to stay with Ogion, to go
wandering through the forests with him, long and far,
learning how to be silent. Yet other cravings were in
him that would not be stilled, the wish for glory, the
will to act. Ogion's seemed a long road towards mastery, a slow bypath to follow, when he might go
sailing before the seawinds straight to the Inmost Sea,
to the Isle of the Wise, where the air was bright with
enchantments and the Archmage walked amidst wonders.

"Master," he said, "I will go to Roke."

So a few days later on a sunny morning of spring
Ogion strode beside him down the steep road from
the Overfell, fifteen miles to the Great Port of Gont.
There at the landgate between carven dragons the

guards of the City of Gont, seeing the mage, knelt with bared swords and welcomed him. They knew him and did him honor by the Prince's order and their own will, for ten years ago Ogion had saved the city from earthquake that would have shaken the towers of the rich down to the ground and closed the channel of the Armed Cliffs with avalanche. He had spoken to the Mountain of Gont, calming it, and had stilled the trembling precipices of the Overfell as one soothes a frightened beast. Ged had heard some talk of this, and now, wondering to see the armed guardsmen kneel to his quiet master, he remembered it. He glanced up almost in fear at this man who had stopped an earthquake; but Ogion's face was quiet as always.

They went down to the quays, where the Harbormaster came hastening to welcome Ogion and ask what service he might do. The mage told him, and at once he named a ship bound for the Inmost Sea aboard which Ged might go as passenger. "Or they will take him as windbringer," he said, "if he has the craft. They have no weatherworker aboard."

"He has some skill with mist and fog, but none with seawinds," the mage said, putting his hand lightly on Ged's shoulder. "Do not try any tricks with the sea and the winds of the sea, Sparrowhawk; you are a landsman still. Harbormaster, what is the ship's name?"

"*Shadow*, from the Andrades, bound to Hort Town with furs and ivories. A good ship, Master Ogion."

The mage's face darkened at the name of the ship, but he said, "So be it. Give this writing to the Warden of the School on Roke, Sparrowhawk. Go with a fair wind. Farewell!"

That was all his parting. He turned away, and went striding up the street away from the quays. Ged stood forlorn and watched his master go.

"Come along, lad," said the Harbormaster, and took him down the waterfront to the pier where *Shadow* was making ready to sail.

It might seem strange that on an island fifty miles
wide, in a village under cliffs that stare out forever on
the sea, a child may grow to manhood never having
stepped in a boat or dipped his finger in salt water,
but so it is. Farmer, goatherd, cattleherd, hunter or
artisan, the landsman looks at the ocean as at a salt
unsteady realm that has nothing to do with him at all.
The village two days' walk from his village is a foreign land, and the island a day's sail from his island is
a mere rumor, misty hills seen across the water, not
solid ground like that he walks on.

So to Ged who had never been down from the
heights of the mountain, the Port of Gont was an
awesome and marvellous place, the great houses and
towers of cut stone and waterfront of piers and docks
and basins and moorages, the seaport where half a
hundred boats and galleys rocked at quayside or lay
hauled up and overturned for repairs or stood out at
anchor in the roadstead with furled sails and closed
oarports, the sailors shouting in strange dialects and
the longshoremen running heavy-laden amongst barrels and boxes and coils of rope and stacks of oars,
the bearded merchants in furred robes conversing
quietly as they picked their way along the slimy
stones above the water, the fishermen unloading their
catch, coopers pounding and shipmakers hammering
and clamsellers singing and shipmasters bellowing,
and beyond all the silent, shining bay. With eyes and
ears and mind bewildered he followed the Harbormaster to the broad dock where *Shadow* was tied up,
and the harbormaster brought him to the master of
the ship.

With few words spoken the ship's master agreed to
take Ged as passenger to Roke, since it was a mage
that asked it; and the Harbormaster left the boy with
him. The master of the *Shadow* was a big man, and
fat, in a red cloak trimmed with pellawi-fur such as
Andradean merchants wear. He never looked at Ged

but asked him in a mighty voice, "Can you work weather, boy?"

"I can."

"Can you bring the wind?"

He had to say he could not, and with that the master told him to find a place out of the way and stay in it.

The oarsmen were coming aboard now, for the ship was to go out into the roadstead before night fell, and sail with the ebb-tide near dawn. There was no place out of the way, but Ged climbed up as well as he could onto the bundled, lashed, and hide-covered cargo in the stern of the ship, and clinging there watched all that passed. The oarsmen came leaping aboard, sturdy men with great arms, while longshoremen rolled water barrels thundering out the dock and stowed them under the rowers' benches. The well-built ship rode low with her burden, yet danced a little on the lapping shore-waves, ready to be gone. Then the steersman took his place at the right of the sternpost, looking forward to the ship's master, who stood on a plank let in at the jointure of the keel with the stem, which was carved as the Old Serpent of Andrad. The master roared his orders hugely, and *Shadow* was untied and towed clear of the docks by two laboring rowboats. Then the master's roar was "Open ports!" and the great oars shot rattling out, fifteen to a side. The rowers bent their strong backs while a lad up beside the master beat the stroke on a drum. Easy as a gull oared by her wings the ship went now, and the noise and hurlyburly of the City fell away suddenly behind. They came out in the silence of the waters of the bay, and over them rose the white peak of the Mountain, seeming to hang above the sea. In a shallow creek in the lee of the southern Armed Cliff the anchor was thrown over, and there they rode the night.

Of the seventy crewmen of the ship some were like Ged very young in years, though all had made their passage into manhood. These lads called him over to share food and drink with them, and were friendly though rough and full of jokes and jibes. They called him Goatherd, of course, because he was Gontish, but they did not go further than that. He was as tall and strong as the fifteen-year-olds, and quick to return either a good word or a jeer; so he made his way among them and even that first night began to live as one of them and learn their work. This suited the ship's officers, for there was no room aboard for idle passengers.

There was little enough room for the crew, and no comfort at all, in an undecked galley crowded with men and gear and cargo; but what was comfort to Ged? He lay that night among corded rolls of pelts from the northern isles and watched the stars of spring above the harbor waters and the little yellow lights of the City astern, and he slept and waked again full of delight. Before dawn the tide turned. They raised anchor and rowed softly out between the Armed Cliffs. As sunrise reddened the Mountain of Gont behind them they raised the high sail and ran southwestward over the Gontish Sea.

Between Barnisk and Torheven they sailed with a light wind, and on the second day came in sight of Havnor, the Great Island, heart and hearth of the Archipelago. For three days they were in sight of the green hills of Havnor as they worked along its eastern coast, but they did not come to shore. Not for many years did Ged set foot on that land or see the white towers of Havnor Great Port at the center of the world.

They lay over one night at Kembermouth, the northern port of Way Island, and the next at a little town on the entrance of Felkway Bay, and the next day passed the northern cape of O and entered the Ebavnor Straits. There they dropped sail and rowed, always with land on either side and always within hail of other ships, great and small, merchants and traders, some bound in from the Outer Reaches with strange cargo after a voyage of years and others that hopped like sparrows from isle to isle of the Inmost Sea. Turning southward out of the crowded Straits they left Havnor astern and sailed between the two fair islands Ark and Ilien, towered and terraced with cities, and then through rain and rising wind began to beat their way across the Inmost Sea to Roke Island.

In the night as the wind freshened to a gale they took down both sail and mast, and the next day, all day, they rowed. The long ship lay steady on the waves and went gallantly, but the steersman at the long steering-sweep in the stern looked into the rain that beat the sea and saw nothing but the rain. They went southwest by the pointing of the magnet, knowing how they went, but not through what waters. Ged heard men speak of the shoal waters north of Roke, and of the Borilous Rocks to the east; others argued that they might be far out of course by now, in the empty waters south of Kamery. Still the wind grew stronger, tearing the edges of the great waves into flying tatters of foam, and still they rowed southwest with the wind behind them. The stints at the oars were shortened, for the labor was very hard; the younger lads were set two to an oar, and Ged took his turn with the others as he had since they left Gont. When they did not row they bailed, for the seas broke heavy on the ship. So they labored among the waves that ran like smoking mountains under the wind, while the rain beat hard and cold on their backs, and the drum thumped through the noise of the storm like a heart thumping.

A man came to take Ged's place at the oar, sending him to the ship's master in the bow. Rainwater dripped from the hem of the master's cloak, but he stood stout as a winebarrel on his bit of decking and looking down at Ged he asked, "Can you abate this wind, lad?"

"No, sir."

"Have you craft with iron?"

He meant, could Ged make the compass-needle point their way to Roke, making the magnet follow not its north but their need. That skill is a secret of the Seamasters, and again Ged must say no.

"Well then," the master bellowed through the wind and rain, "you must find some ship to take you back to Roke from Hort Town. Roke must be west of us now, and only wizardry could bring us there through this sea. We must keep south."

Ged did not like this, for he had heard the sailors talk of Hort Town, how it was a lawless place, full of evil traffic, where men were often taken and sold into slavery in the South Reach. Returning to his labor at the oar he pulled away with his companion, a sturdy Andradean lad, and heard the drum beat the stroke and saw the lantern hung on the stern bob and flicker as the wind plucked it about, a tormented fleck of light in the rain-lashed dusk. He kept looking to westward, as often as he could in the heavy rhythm of pulling the oar. And as the ship rose on a high swell he saw for a moment over the dark smoking water a light between clouds, as it might be the last gleam of sunset: but this was a clear light, not red.

His oar-mate had not seen it, but he called it out. The steersman watched for it on each rise of the great waves, and saw it as Ged saw it again, but shouted back that it was only the setting sun. Then Ged called to one of the lads that was bailing to take his place on the bench a minute, and made his way forward again along the encumbered aisle between the benches, and catching hold of the carved prow to keep from being pitched overboard he shouted up to the master, "Sir! that light to the west is Roke Island!"

"I saw no light," the master roared, but even as he spoke Ged flung out his arm pointing, and all saw the light gleam clear in the west over the heaving scud and tumult of the sea.

Not for his passenger's sake, but to save his ship

from the peril of the storm, the master shouted at
once to the steersman to head westward toward the
light. But he said to Ged, "Boy, you speak like a
Seamaster, but I tell you if you lead us wrong in this
weather I will throw you over to swim to Roke!"

Now instead of running before the storm they must
row across the wind's way, and it was hard: waves
striking the ship abeam pushed her always south of
their new course, and rolled her, and filled her with
water so that bailing must be ceaseless, and the oarsmen must watch lest the ship rolling should lift their
oars out of water as they pulled and so pitch them
down among the benches. It was nearly dark under
the stormclouds, but now and again they made out
the light to the west, enough to set course by, and so
struggled on. At last the wind dropped a little, and
the light grew broad before them. They rowed on,
and they came as it were through a curtain, between
one oarstroke and the next running out of the storm
into a clear air, where the light of after-sunset glowed
in the sky and on the sea. Over the foam-crested
waves they saw not far off a high, round, green hill,
and beneath it a town built on a small bay where
boats lay at anchor, all in peace.

The steersman leaning on his long sweep turned his
head and called, "Sir! is this true land or a witchery?"

"Keep her as she goes, you witless woodenhead!
Row, you spineless slave-sons! That's Thwil Bay and
the Knoll of Roke, as any fool could see! Row!"

So to the beat of the drum they rowed wearily into
the bay. There it was still, so that they could hear the
voices of people up in the town, and a bell ringing,
and only far off the hiss and roaring of the storm.
Clouds hung dark to north and east and south a mile
off all about the island. But over Roke stars were
coming out one by one in a clear and quiet sky.

# 3 The School for Wizards

Ged slept that night aboard *Shadow*, and early in the morning parted with those first sea-comrades of his, they shouting good wishes cheerily after him as he went up the docks. The town of Thwil is not large, its high houses huddling close over a few steep narrow streets. To Ged, however, it seemed a city, and not knowing where to go he asked the first townsman of Thwil he met where he would find the Warder of the School on Roke. The man looked at him sidelong a while and said, "The wise don't need to ask, the fool asks in vain," and so went on along the street. Ged went uphill till he came out into a square, rimmed on three sides by the houses with their sharp slate roofs and on the fourth side by the wall of a great building whose few small windows were higher than the chimneytops of the houses: a fort or castle it seemed, built of mighty grey blocks of stone. In the square beneath it market-booths were set up and there was some coming and going of people. Ged asked his question of an old woman with a basket of mussels, and she

33

replied, "You cannot always find the Warder where he is, but sometimes you find him where he is not," and went on crying her mussels to sell.

In the great building, near one corner, there was a mean little door of wood. Ged went to this and knocked loud. To the old man who opened the door he said, "I bear a letter from the Mage Ogion of Gont to the Warder of the School on this island. I want to find the Warder, but I will not hear more riddles and scoffing!"

"This is the School," the old man said mildly. "I am the doorkeeper. Enter if you can."

Ged stepped forward. It seemed to him that he had passed through the doorway: yet he stood outside on the pavement where he had stood before.

Once more he stepped forward, and once more he remained standing outside the door. The doorkeeper, inside, watched him with mild eyes.

Ged was not so much baffled as angry, for this seemed like a further mockery to him. With voice and hand he made the Opening spell which his aunt had taught him long ago; it was the prize among all her stock of spells, and he wove it well now. But it was only a witch's charm, and the power that held this doorway was not moved at all.

When that failed Ged stood a long while there on the pavement. At last he looked at the old man who waited inside. "I cannot enter," he said unwillingly, "unless you help me."

The doorkeeper answered, "Say your name."

Then again Ged stood still a while; for a man never speaks his own name aloud, until more than his life's safety is at stake.

"I am Ged," he said aloud. Stepping forward then he entered the open doorway. Yet it seemed to him that though the light was behind him, a shadow followed him in at his heels.

He saw also as he turned that the doorway through which he had come was not plain wood as he had thought, but ivory without joint or seam: it was cut, as he knew later, from a tooth of the Great Dragon. The door that the old man closed behind him was of polished horn, through which the daylight shone dimly, and on its inner face was carved the Thousand-Leaved Tree.

"Welcome to this house, lad," the doorkeeper said, and without saying more led him through halls and corridors to an open court far inside the walls of the building. The court was partly paved with stone, but was roofless, and on a grassplot a fountain played under young trees in the sunlight. There Ged waited alone some while. He stood still, and his heart beat hard, for it seemed to him that he felt presences and powers at work unseen about him here, and he knew that this place was built not only of stone but of magic stronger than stone. He stood in the innermost room of the House of the Wise, and it was open to the sky. Then suddenly he was aware of a man clothed in white who watched him through the falling water of the fountain.

As their eyes met, a bird sang aloud in the branches of the tree. In that moment Ged understood the singing of the bird, and the language of the water falling in the basin of the fountain, and the shape of the clouds, and the beginning and end of the wind that stirred the leaves: it seemed to him that he himself was a word spoken by the sunlight.

Then that moment passed, and he and the world were as before, or almost as before. He went forward to kneel before the Archmage, holding out to him the letter written by Ogion.

The Archmage Nemmerle, Warder of Roke, was an old man, older it was said than any man then living. His voice quavered like the bird's voice when he spoke, welcoming Ged kindly. His hair and beard and robe were white, and he seemed as if all darkness and heaviness had been leached out of him by the slow usage of the years, leaving him white and worn as driftwood that has been a century adrift. "My eyes are old, I cannot read what your master writes," he said in his quavering voice. "Read me the letter, lad."

So Ged made out and read aloud the writing, which was in Hardic runes, and said no more than this: *Lord Nemmerle! I send you one who will be greatest of the wizards of Gont, if the wind blow true.* This was signed, not with Ogion's true name which Ged had never yet learned, but with Ogion's rune, the Closed Mouth.

"He who holds the earthquake on a leash has sent you, for which be doubly welcome. Young Ogion was dear to me, when he came here from Gont. Now tell me of the seas and portents of your voyage, lad."

"A fair passage, Lord, but for the storm yesterday."

"What ship brought you here?"

"*Shadow*, trading from the Andrades."

"Whose will sent you here?"

"My own."

The Archmage looked at Ged and looked away, and began to speak in a tongue that Ged did not understand, mumbling as will an old old man whose wits go wandering among the years and islands. Yet in among his mumbling there were words of what the bird had sung and what the water had said falling. He was not laying a spell and yet there was a power in his voice that moved Ged's mind so that the boy was bewildered, and for an instant seemed to behold himself standing in a strange vast desert place alone among shadows. Yet all along he was in the sunlit court, hearing the fountain fall.

A great black bird, a raven of Osskil, came walking over the stone terrace and the grass. It came to the hem of the Archmage's robe and stood there all black with its dagger beak and eyes like pebbles, staring sidelong at Ged. It pecked three times on the white staff Nemmerle leaned on, and the old wizard ceased his muttering, and smiled. "Run and play, lad," he said at last as to a little child. Ged knelt again on one knee to him. When he rose, the Archmage was gone. Only the raven stood eyeing him, its beak outstretched as if to peck the vanished staff.

It spoke, in what Ged guessed might be the speech of Osskil. "Terrenon ussbuk!" it said croaking. "Terrenon ussbuk orrek!" And it strutted off as it had come.

Ged turned to leave the courtyard, wondering where he should go. Under the archway he was met by a tall youth who greeted him very courteously, bowing his head. "I am called Jasper, Enwit's son of the Domain of Eolg on Havnor Isle. I am at your service today, to show you about the Great House and answer your questions as I can. How shall I call you, Sir?"

Now it seemed to Ged, a mountain villager who had never been among the sons of rich merchants and noblemen, that this fellow was scoffing at him with his "service" and his "Sir" and his bowing and scraping. He answered shortly, "Sparrowhawk, they call me."

The other waited a moment as if expecting some more mannerly response, and getting none straightened up and turned a little aside. He was two or three years older than Ged, very tall, and he moved and carried himself with stiff grace, posing (Ged thought) like a dancer. He wore a grey cloak with hood thrown back. The first place he took Ged was the wardrobe room, where as a student of the school Ged might find himself another such cloak that fitted him, and any other clothing he might need. He put on the dark-grey cloak he had chosen, and Jasper said, "Now you are one of us."

Jasper had a way of smiling faintly as he spoke which made Ged look for a jeer hidden in his polite words. "Do clothes make the mage?" he answered, sullen.

"No," said the older boy. "Though I have heard that manners make the man.—Where now?"

"Where you will. I do not know the house."

Jasper took him down the corridors of the Great House showing him the open courts and the roofed halls, the Room of Shelves where the books of lore and rune-tomes were kept, the great Hearth Hall where all the school gathered on festival days, and upstairs, in the towers and under the roofs, the small cells where the students and Masters slept. Ged's was in the South Tower, with a window looking down over the steep roofs of Thwil town to the sea. Like the other sleeping-cells it had no furnishing but a straw-filled mattress in the corner. "We live very plain here," said Jasper. "But I expect you won't mind that."

"I'm used to it." Presently, trying to show himself an equal of this polite disdainful youth, he added, "I suppose you weren't, when you first came."

Jasper looked at him, and his look said without words, "What could you possibly know about what I, son of the Lord of the Domain of Eolg on the Isle of Havnor, am or am not used to?" What Jasper said aloud was simply, "Come on this way."

A gong had been rung while they were upstairs, and they came down to eat the noon meal at the Long Table of the refectory, along with a hundred or more boys and young men. Each waited on himself, joking with the cooks through the window-hatches of the kitchen that opened into the refectory, loading his plate from great bowls of food that steamed on the sills, sitting where he pleased at the Long Table. "They say," Jasper told Ged, "that no matter how many sit at this table, there is always room." Certainly there was room both for many noisy groups of boys talking and eating mightily, and for older fellows, their grey cloaks clasped with silver at the neck, who sat more quietly by pairs or alone, with grave, pondering faces, as if they had much to think about. Jasper took Ged to sit with a heavyset fellow called Vetch, who said nothing much but shovelled in his

food with a will. He had the accent of the East
Reach, and was very dark of skin, not red-brown like
Ged and Jasper and most folk of the Archipelago, but
black-brown. He was plain, and his manners were not
polished. He grumbled about the dinner when he had
finished it, but then turning to Ged said, "At least it's
not illusion, like so much around here; it sticks to
your ribs." Ged did not know what he meant, but he
felt a certain liking for him, and was glad when after
the meal he stayed with them.

They went down into the town, that Ged might
learn his way about it. Few and short as were the
streets of Thwil, they turned and twisted curiously
among the high-roofed houses, and the way was easy
to lose. It was a strange town, and strange also its
people, fishermen and workmen and artisans like any
others, but so used to the sorcery that is ever at play
on the Isle of the Wise that they seemed half sorcerers themselves. They talked (as Ged had learned) in
riddles, and not one of them would blink to see a boy
turn into a fish or a house fly up into the air, but
knowing it for a schoolboy prank would go on cob-
bling shoes or cutting up mutton, unconcerned.

Coming up past the Back Door and around through
the gardens of the Great House, the three boys
crossed the clear-running Thwilburn on a wooden
bridge and went on northward among woods and pastures. The path climbed and wound. They passed oak-
groves where shadows lay thick for all the brightness
of the sun. There was one grove not far away to the
left that Ged could never quite see plainly. The path
never reached it, though it always seemed to be
about to. He could not even make out what kind of
trees they were. Vetch, seeing him gazing, said softly,
"That is the Immanent Grove. We can't come there,
yet. . . ."

In the hot sunlit pastures yellow flowers bloomed.
"Sparkweed," said Jasper. "They grow where the
wind dropped the ashes of burning Ilien, when Er-

reth-Akbe defended the Inward Isles from the Fire-lord." He blew on a withered flowerhead, and the seeds shaken loose went up on the wind like sparks of fire in the sun.

The path led them up and around the base of a great green hill, round and treeless, the hill that Ged had seen from the ship as they entered the charmed waters of Roke Island. On the hillside Jasper halted. "At home in Havnor I heard much about Gontish wizardry, and always in praise, so that I've wanted for a long time to see the manner of it. Here now we have a Gontishman; and we stand on the slopes of Roke Knoll, whose roots go down to the center of the earth. All spells are strong here. Play us a trick, Spar-rowhawk. Show us your style."

Ged, confused and taken aback, said nothing.

"Later on, Jasper," Vetch said in his plain way. "Let him be a while."

"He has either skill or power, or the doorkeeper wouldn't have let him in. Why shouldn't he show it, now as well as later? Right, Sparrowhawk?"

"I have both skill and power," Ged said. "Show me what kind of thing you're talking about."

"Illusions, of course—tricks, games of seeming. Like this!"

Pointing his finger Jasper spoke a few strange words, and where he pointed on the hillside among the green grasses a little thread of water trickled, and grew, and now a spring gushed out and the water went running down the hill. Ged put his hand in the stream and it felt wet, drank of it and it was cool. Yet for all that it would quench no thirst, being but illusion. Jasper with another word stopped the water, and the grasses waved dry in the sunlight. "Now you, Vetch," he said with his cool smile.

Vetch scratched his head and looked glum, but he took up a bit of earth in his hand and began to sing tunelessly over it, molding it with his dark fingers and shaping it, pressing it, stroking it: and suddenly it was a small creature like a bumblebee or furry fly, that flew humming off over Roke Knoll, and vanished.

Ged stood staring, crestfallen. What did he know but mere village witchery, spells to call goats, cure warts, move loads or mend pots?

"I do no such tricks as these," he said. That was enough for Vetch, who was for going on; but Jasper said, "Why don't you?"

"Sorcery is not a game. We Gontishmen do not play it for pleasure or praise," Ged answered haughtily.

"What do you play it for," Jasper inquired, "—money?"

"No!—" But he could not think of anything more to say that would hide his ignorance and save his pride. Jasper laughed, not ill-humoredly, and went on, leading them on around Roke Knoll. And Ged followed, sullen and sore-hearted, knowing he had behaved like a fool, and blaming Jasper for it.

That night as he lay wrapped in his cloak on the mattress in his cold unlit cell of stone, in the utter silence of the Great House of Roke, the strangeness of the place and the thought of all the spells and sorceries that had been worked there began to come over him heavily. Darkness surrounded him, dread filled him. He wished he were anywhere else but Roke. But Vetch came to the door, a little bluish ball of werelight nodding over his head to light the way, and asked if he could come in and talk a while. He asked Ged about Gont, and then spoke fondly of his own home isles of the East Reach, telling how the smoke of village hearthfires is blown across that quiet sea at evening between the small islands with funny names: Korp, Kopp, and Holp, Venway and Vemish, Iffish, Koppish, and Sneg. When he sketched the shapes of those lands on the stones of the floor with his finger to show Ged how they lay, the lines he drew shone dim as if drawn with a stick of silver for a while before they faded. Vetch had been three years at the School, and soon would be made Sorcerer; he thought no more of performing the lesser arts of magic than a bird thinks of flying. Yet a greater, unlearned skill he possessed, which was the art of kindness. That night, and always from then on, he offered and gave Ged friendship, a sure and open friendship which Ged could not help but return.

Yet Vetch was also friendly to Jasper, who had made Ged into a fool that first day on Roke Knoll. Ged would not forget this, nor, it seemed, would Jasper, who always spoke to him with a polite voice and a mocking smile. Ged's pride would not be slighted or condescended to. He swore to prove to Jasper, and to all the rest of them among whom Jasper was something of a leader, how great his power really was— some day. For none of them, for all their clever tricks, had saved a village by wizardry. Of none of them had Ogion written that he would be the greatest wizard of Gont.

So bolstering up his pride, he set all his strong will on the work they gave him, the lessons and crafts and histories and skills taught by the grey-cloaked Masters of Roke, who were called the Nine.

Part of each day he studied with the Master Chanter, learning the Deeds of heroes and the Lays of wisdom, beginning with the oldest of all songs, the *Creation of Éa*. Then with a dozen other lads he would practice with the Master Windkey at arts of wind and weather. Whole bright days of spring and early summer they spent out in Roke Bay in light catboats, practising steering by word, and stilling waves, and speaking to the world's wind, and raising up the magewind. These are very intricate skills, and frequently Ged's head got whacked by the swinging boom as the boat jibed under a wind suddenly blowing backwards, or his boat and another collided though they had the whole bay to navigate in, or all three boys in his boat went swimming unexpectedly as the boat was swamped by a huge, unintended wave. There were quieter expeditions ashore, other days, with the Master Herbal who taught the ways and properties of things that grow; and the Master Hand taught sleight and jugglery and the lesser arts of Changing.

At all these studies Ged was apt, and within a month was bettering lads who had been a year at Roke before him. Especially the tricks of illusion came to him so easily that it seemed he had been born knowing them and needed only to be reminded. The Master Hand was a gentle and light-hearted old man, who had endless delight in the wit and beauty of the crafts he taught; Ged soon felt no awe of him, but asked him for this spell and that spell, and always the Master smiled and showed him what he wanted. But one day, having it in mind to put Jasper to shame at last, Ged said to the Master Hand in the Court of Seeming, "Sir, all these charms are much the same; knowing one, you know them all. And as soon as the spell-weaving ceases, the illusion vanishes. Now if I make a pebble into a diamond—" and he did so with a word and a flick of his wrist—"what must I do to make that diamond remain diamond? How is the changing-spell locked, and made to last?"

The Master Hand looked at the jewel that glittered on Ged's palm, bright as the prize of a dragon's hoard. The old Master murmured one word, *"Tolk,"* and there lay the pebble, no jewel but a rough grey bit of rock. The Master took it and held it out on his own hand. "This is a rock; *tolk* in the True Speech," he said, looking mildly up at Ged now. "A bit of the stone of which Roke Isle is made, a little bit of the dry land on which men live. It is itself. It is part of the world. By the Illusion-Change you can make it look like a diamond—or a flower or a fly or an eye or a flame—" The rock flickered from shape to shape as he named them, and returned to rock. "But that is mere seeming. Illusion fools the beholder's senses; it makes him see and hear and feel that the thing is changed. But it does not change the thing. To change this rock into a jewel, you must change its true name. And to do that, my son, even to so small a scrap of the world, is to change the world. It can be done. Indeed it can be done. It is the art of the Master Changer, and you will learn it, when you are ready to learn it. But you must not change one thing, one pebble, one grain of sand, until you know what good and evil will follow on that act. The world is in balance, in Equilibrium. A wizard's power of Changing and of Summoning can shake the balance of the world. It is dangerous, that power. It is most perilous. It must follow knowledge, and serve need. To light a candle is to cast a shadow. . . ."

He looked down at the pebble again. "A rock is a good thing, too, you know," he said, speaking less gravely. "If the Isles of Earthsea were all made of diamond, we'd lead a hard life here. Enjoy illusions, lad, and let the rocks be rocks." He smiled, but Ged left dissatisfied. Press a mage for his secrets and he would always talk, like Ogion, about balance, and danger, and the dark. But surely a wizard, one who had gone past these childish tricks of illusion to the true arts of Summoning and Change, was powerful enough to do what he pleased, and balance the world as seemed best to him, and drive back darkness with his own light.

In the corridor he met Jasper, who, since Ged's accomplishments began to be praised about the School, spoke to him in a way that seemed more friendly, but was more scoffing. "You look gloomy, Sparrowhawk," he said now, "did your juggling-charms go wrong?"

Seeking as always to put himself on equal footing with Jasper, Ged answered the question ignoring its ironic tone. "I'm sick of juggling," he said, "sick of these illusion-tricks, fit only to amuse idle lords in their castles and Domains. The only true magic they've taught me yet on Roke is making werelight, and some weatherworking. The rest is mere foolery."

"Even foolery is dangerous," said Jasper, "in the hands of a fool."

At that Ged turned as if he had been slapped, and took a step towards Jasper; but the older boy smiled as if he had not intended any insult, nodded his head in his stiff, graceful way, and went on.

Standing there with rage in his heart, looking after Jasper, Ged swore to himself to outdo his rival, and not in some mere illusion-match but in a test of power. He would prove himself, and humiliate Jasper. He would not let the fellow stand there looking down at him, graceful, disdainful, hateful.

Ged did not stop to think why Jasper might hate him. He only knew why he hated Jasper. The other prentices had soon learned they could seldom match themselves against Ged either in sport or in earnest, and they said of him, some in praise and some in spite, "He's a wizard born, he'll never let you beat him." Jasper alone neither praised him nor avoided him, but simply looked down at him, smiling slightly. And therefore Jasper stood alone as his rival, who must be put to shame.

He did not see, or would not see, that in this rivalry, which he clung to and fostered as part of his own pride, there was anything of the danger, the darkness, of which the Master Hand had mildly warned him.

When he was not moved by pure rage, he knew very well that he was as yet no match for Jasper, or any of the older boys, and so he kept at his work and went on as usual. At the end of summer the work was slackened somewhat, so there was more time for sport: spell-boat races down in the harbor, feats of illusion in the courts of the Great House, and in the long evenings, in the groves, wild games of hide-and-seek where hiders and seeker were both invisible and only voices moved laughing and calling among the trees, following and dodging the quick, faint were-lights. Then as autumn came they set to their tasks afresh, practising new magic. So Ged's first months at Roke went by fast, full of passions and wonders.

In winter it was different. He was sent with seven other boys across Roke Island to the farthest northmost cape, where stands the Isolate Tower. There by himself lived the Master Namer, who was called by a name that had no meaning in any language, Kurremkarmerruk. No farm or dwelling lay within miles of the Tower. Grim it stood above the northern cliffs, grey were the clouds over the seas of winter, endless the lists and ranks and rounds of names that the Namer's eight pupils must learn. Amongst them in the Tower's high room Kurremkarmerruk sat on a high seat, writing down lists of names that must be learned before the ink faded at midnight leaving the parchment blank again. It was cold and half-dark and always silent there except for the scratching of the Master's pen and the sighing, maybe, of a student who must learn before midnight the name of every cape, point, bay, sound, inlet, channel, harbor, shallows, reef and rock of the shores of Lossow, a little islet of the Pelnish Sea. If the student complained the Master might say nothing, but lengthen the list; or he might say, "He who would be Seamaster must know the true name of every drop of water in the sea."

Ged sighed sometimes, but he did not complain. He saw that in this dusty and fathomless matter of learning the true name of every place, thing, and being, the power he wanted lay like a jewel at the bottom of a dry well. For magic consists in this, the true naming of a thing. So Kurremkarmerruk had said to them, once, their first night in the Tower; he never repeated it, but Ged did not forget his words. "Many a mage of great power," he had said, "has spent his whole life to find out the name of one single thing—one single lost or hidden name. And still the lists are not finished. Nor will they be, till world's end. Listen, and you will see why. In the world under the sun, and in the other world that has no sun, there is much that has nothing to do with men and men's speech, and there are powers beyond our power. But magic, true magic, is worked only by those beings who speak the Hardic tongue of Earthsea, or the Old Speech from which it grew.

"That is the language dragons speak, and the language Segoy spoke who made the islands of the world, and the language of our lays and songs, spells, enchantments, and invocations. Its words lie hidden and changed among our Hardic words. We call the foam on waves *sukien*: that word is made from two words of the Old Speech, *suk*, feather, and *inien*, the sea. Feather of the sea, is foam. But you cannot charm the foam calling it *sukien*; you must use its own true name in the Old Speech, which is *essa*. Any witch knows a few of these words in the Old Speech, and a mage knows many. But there are many more, and some have been lost over the ages, and some have been hidden, and some are known only to dragons and to the Old Powers of Earth, and some are known to no living creature; and no man could learn them all. For there is no end to that language.

"Here is the reason. The sea's name is *inien*, well and good. But what we call the Inmost Sea has its own name also in the Old Speech. Since no thing can have two true names, *inien* can mean only 'all the sea except the Inmost Sea.' And of course it does not mean even that, for there are seas and bays and straits beyond counting that bear names of their own. So if some Mage-Seamaster were mad enough to try to lay a spell of storm or calm over all the ocean, his spell must say not only that word *inien*, but the name of every stretch and bit and part of the sea through all the Archipelago and all the Outer Reaches and beyond to where names cease. Thus, that which gives us the power to work magic, sets the limits of that power. A mage can control only what is near him, what he can name exactly and wholly. And this is well. If it were not so, the wickedness of the powerful or the folly of the wise would long ago have sought to change what cannot be changed, and Equilibrium would fail. The unbalanced sea would overwhelm the islands where we perilously dwell, and in the old silence all voices and all names would be lost."

Ged thought long on these words, and they went deep in his understanding. Yet the majesty of the task could not make the work of that long year in the Tower less hard and dry; and at the end of the year Kurremkarmerruk said to him, "You have made a good beginning." But no more. Wizards speak truth, and it was true that all the mastery of Names that Ged had toiled to win that year was the mere start of what he must go on learning all his life. He was let go from the Isolate Tower sooner than those who had come with him, for he had learned quicker; but that was all the praise he got.

He walked south across the island alone in the early winter, along townless empty roads. As night came on it rained. He said no charm to keep the rain off him, for the weather of Roke was in the hands of the Master Windkey and might not be tampered with. He took shelter under a great pendick-tree, and lying there wrapped in his cloak he thought of his old master Ogion, who might still be on his autumn wanderings over the heights of Gont, sleeping out with leafless branches for a roof and falling rain for house-walls. That made Ged smile, for he found the thought of Ogion always a comfort to him. He fell asleep with a peaceful heart, there in the cold darkness full of the whisper of water. At dawn waking he lifted his head; the rain had ceased; he saw, sheltered in the folds of his cloak, a little animal curled up asleep which had crept there for warmth. He wondered, seeing it, for it was a rare strange beast, an otak.

These creatures are found only on four southern isles of the Archipelago, Roke, Ensmer, Pody and Wathort. They are small and sleek, with broad faces, and fur dark brown or brindle, and great bright eyes.

Their teeth are cruel and their temper fierce, so they are not made pets of. They have no call or cry or any voice. Ged stroked this one, and it woke and yawned, showing a small brown tongue and white teeth, but it was not afraid. "Otak," he said, and then remembering the thousand names of beasts he had learned in the Tower he called it by its true name in the Old Speech, "Hoeg! Do you want to come with me?"

The otak sat itself down on his open hand, and began to wash its fur.

He put it up on his shoulder in the folds of his hood, and there it rode. Sometimes during the day it jumped down and darted off into the woods, but it always came back to him, once with a woodmouse it had caught. He laughed and told it to eat the mouse, for he was fasting, this night being the Festival of Sunreturn. So he came in the wet dusk past Roke Knoll, and saw bright werelights playing in the rain over the roofs of the Great House, and he entered there and was welcomed by his Masters and companions in the firelit hall.

It was like a homecoming to Ged, who had no home to which he could ever return. He was happy to see so many faces he knew, and happiest to see Vetch come forward to greet him with a wide smile on his dark face. He had missed his friend this year more than he knew. Vetch had been made sorcerer this fall and was a prentice no more, but that set no barrier between them. They fell to talking at once, and it seemed to Ged that he said more to Vetch in that first hour than he had said during the whole long year at the Isolate Tower.

The otak still rode his shoulder, nestling in the fold of his hood as they sat at dinner at long tables set up for the festival in the Hearth Hall. Vetch marvelled at the little creature, and once put up his hand to stroke it, but the otak snapped its sharp teeth at him. He laughed. "They say, Sparrowhawk, that a man favored by a wild beast is a man to whom the Old

Powers of stone and spring will speak in human voice."

"They say Gontish wizards often keep familiars," said Jasper, who sat on the other side of Vetch. "Our Lord Nemmerle has his raven, and songs say the Red Mage of Ark led a wild boar on a gold chain. But I never heard of any sorcerer keeping a rat in his hood!"

At that they all laughed, and Ged laughed with them. It was a merry night and he was joyful to be there in the warmth and merriment, keeping festival with his companions. But, like all Jasper ever said to him, the jest set his teeth on edge.

That night the Lord of O was a guest of the school, himself a sorcerer of renown. He had been a pupil of the Archmage, and returned sometimes to Roke for the Winter Festival or the Long Dance in summer. With him was his lady, slender and young, bright as new copper, her black hair crowned with opals. It was seldom that any woman sat in the halls of the Great House, and some of the old Masters looked at her sidelong, disapproving. But the young men looked at her with all their eyes.

"For such a one," said Vetch to Ged, "I could work vast enchantments. . . ." He sighed, and laughed.

"She's only a woman," Ged replied.

"The Princess Elfarran was only a woman," said Vetch, "and for her sake all Enlad was laid waste, and the Hero-Mage of Havnor died, and the island Soléa sank beneath the sea."

"Old tales," says Ged. But then he too began to look at the Lady of O, wondering if indeed this was such mortal beauty as the old tales told of.

The Master Chanter had sung the *Deed of the Young King*, and all together had sung the Winter Carol. Now when there was a little pause before they all rose from the tables, Jasper got up and went to the table nearest the hearth, where the Archmage and the guests and Masters sat, and he spoke to the Lady of O. Jasper was no longer a boy but a young man, tall and comely, with his cloak clasped at the neck with silver; for he also had been made sorcerer this year, and the silver clasp was the token of it. The lady smiled at what he said and the opals shone in her black hair, radiant. Then, the Masters nodding benign consent, Jasper worked an illusion-charm for her. A white tree he made spring up from the stone floor. Its branches touched the high roofbeams of the hall, and on every twig of every branch a golden apple shone, each a sun, for it was the Year-Tree. A bird flew among the branches suddenly, all white with a tail like a fall of snow, and the golden apples dimming turned to seeds, each one a drop of crystal. These falling from the tree with a sound like rain, all at once there came a sweet fragrance, while the tree, swaying, put forth leaves of rosy fire and white flowers like stars. So the illusion faded. The Lady of O cried out with pleasure, and bent her shining head to the young sorcerer in praise of his mastery. "Come with us, live with us in O-tokne—can he not come, my lord?" she asked, childlike, of her stern husband. But Jasper said only, "When I have learned skills worthy of my Masters here and worthy of your praise, my lady, then I will gladly come, and serve you ever gladly."

So he pleased all there, except Ged. Ged joined his voice to the praises, but not his heart. "I could have done better," he said to himself, in bitter envy; and all the joy of the evening was darkened for him, after that.

# 4 The Loosing of the Shadow

That spring Ged saw little of either Vetch or Jasper, for they being sorcerers studied now with the Master Patterner in the secrecy of the Immanent Grove, where no prentice might set foot. Ged stayed in the Great House, working with the Masters at all the skills practised by sorcerers, those who work magic but carry no staff: windbringing, weatherworking, finding and binding, and the arts of spellsmiths and spellwrights, tellers, chanters, healalls and herbalists. At night alone in his sleeping-cell, a little ball of werelight burning above the book in place of lamp or candle, he studied the Further Runes and the Runes of Éa, which are used in the Great Spells. All these crafts came easy to him, and it was rumored among the students that this Master or that had said that the Gontish lad was the quickest student that had ever been at Roke, and tales grew up concerning the otak, which was said to be a disguised spirit who whispered wisdom in Ged's ear, and it was even said that the Archmage's raven had hailed Ged at his arrival as

"Archmage to be." Whether or not they believed such stories, and whether or not they liked Ged, most of his companions admired him, and were eager to follow him when the rare wild mood came over him and he joined them to lead their games on the lengthening evenings of spring. But for the most part he was all work and pride and temper, and held himself apart. Among them all, Vetch being absent, he had no friend, and never knew he wanted one.

He was fifteen, very young to learn any of the High Arts of wizard or mage, those who carry the staff; but he was so quick to learn all the arts of illusion that the Master Changer, himself a young man, soon began to teach him apart from the others, and to tell him about the true Spells of Shaping. He explained how, if a thing is really to be changed into another thing, it must be renamed for as long as the spell lasts, and he told how this affects the names and natures of things surrounding the transformed thing. He spoke of the perils of changing, above all when the wizard transforms his own shape and thus is liable to be caught in his own spell. Little by little, drawn on by the boy's sureness of understanding, the young Master began to do more than merely tell him of these mysteries. He taught him first one and then another of the Great Spells of Change, and he gave him the Book of Shaping to study. This he did without knowledge of the Archmage, and unwisely, yet he meant no harm.

Ged worked also with the Master Summoner now, but that Master was a stern man, aged and hardened by the deep and somber wizardry he taught. He dealt with no illusion, only true magic, the summoning of such energies as light, and heat, and the force that draws the magnet, and those forces men perceive as weight, form, color, sound: real powers, drawn from the immense fathomless energies of the universe, which no man's spells or uses could exhaust or unbalance. The weatherworker's and seamaster's calling

upon wind and water were crafts already known to
his pupils, but it was he who showed them why the
true wizard uses such spells only at need, since to
summon up such earthly forces is to change the earth
of which they are a part. "Rain on Roke may be
drouth in Osskil," he said, "and a calm in the East
Reach may be storm and ruin in the West, unless you
know what you are about."

As for the calling of real things and living people,
and the raising up of spirits of the dead, and the invocations of the Unseen, those spells which are the
height of the Summoner's art and the mage's power,
those he scarcely spoke of to them. Once or twice
Ged tried to lead him to talk a little of such mysteries, but the Master was silent, looking at him long
and grimly, till Ged grew uneasy and said no more.

Sometimes indeed he was uneasy working even
such lesser spells as the Summoner taught him. There
were certain runes on certain pages of the Lore-Book
that seemed familiar to him, though he did not
remember in what book he had ever seen them before. There were certain phrases that must be said in
spells of Summoning that he did not like to say. They
made him think, for an instant, of shadows in a dark
room, of a shut door and shadows reaching out to
him from the corner by the door. Hastily he put such
thoughts or memories aside and went on. These moments of fear and darkness, he said to himself, were
the shadows merely of his ignorance. The more he
learned, the less he would have to fear, until finally in
his full power as Wizard he needed fear nothing in
the world, nothing at all.

In the second month of that summer all the school
gathered again at the Great House to celebrate the
Moon's Night and the Long Dance, which that year
fell together as one festival of two nights, which hap-
pens but once in fifty-two years. All the first night,
the shortest night of full moon of the year, flutes
played out in the fields, and the narrow streets of

Thwil were full of drums and torches, and the sound of singing went out over the moonlit waters of Roke Bay. As the sun rose next morning the Chanters of Roke began to sing the long *Deed of Erreth-Akbe*, which tells how the white towers of Havnor were built, and of Erreth-Akbe's journeys from the Old Island, Éa, through all the Archipelago and the Reaches, until at last in the uttermost West Reach on the edge of the Open Sea he met the dragon Orm; and his bones in shattered armor lie among the dragon's bones on the shore of lonely Selidor, but his sword set atop the highest tower of Havnor still burns red in the sunset above the Inmost Sea. When the chant was finished the Long Dance began. Townsfolk and Masters and students and farmers all together, men and women, danced in the warm dust and dusk down all the roads of Roke to the sea-beaches, to the beat of drums and drone of pipes and flutes. Straight out into the sea they danced, under the moon one night past full, and the music was lost in the breakers' sound. As the east grew light they came back up the beaches and the roads, the drums silent and only the flutes playing soft and shrill. So it was done on every island of the Archipelago that night: one dance, one music binding together the sea-divided lands.

When the Long Dance was over most people slept the day away, and gathered again at evening to eat and drink. There was a group of young fellows, prentices and sorcerers, who had brought their supper out from the refectory to hold private feast in a courtyard of the Great House: Vetch, Jasper, and Ged were there, and six or seven others, and some young lads released briefly from the Isolate Tower, for this festival had brought even Kurremkarmerruk out. They were all eating and laughing and playing such tricks out of pure frolic as might be the marvel of a king's court. One boy had lighted the court with a hundred stars of werelight, colored like jewels, that swung in a slow netted procession between them and the real stars; and a pair of boys were playing bowls with balls of green flame and bowling-pins that leaped and hopped away as the ball came near; and all the while Vetch sat cross-legged, eating roast chicken, up in mid-air. One of the younger boys tried to pull him down to earth, but Vetch merely drifted up a little higher, out of reach, and sat calmly smiling on the air. Now and then he tossed away a chicken bone, which turned to an owl and flew hooting among the netted star-lights. Ged shot breadcrumb arrows after the owls and brought them down, and when they touched the ground there they lay, bone and crumb, all illusion gone. Ged also tried to join Vetch up in the middle of the air, but lacking the key of the spell he had to flap his arms to keep aloft, and they were all laughing at his flights and flaps and bumps. He kept up his foolishness for the laughter's sake, laughing with them, for after those two long nights of dance and moonlight and music and magery he was in a fey and wild mood, ready for whatever might come.

He came lightly down on his feet just beside Jasper at last, and Jasper, who never laughed aloud, moved away saying, "The Sparrowhawk that can't fly . . ."

"Is jasper a precious stone?" Ged returned, grinning. "O Jewel among sorcerers, O Gem of Havnor, sparkle for us!"

The lad that had set the lights dancing sent one down to dance and glitter about Jasper's head. Not quite as cool as usual, frowning, Jasper brushed the light away and snuffed it out with one gesture. "I am sick of boys and noise and foolishness," he said.

"You're getting middle-aged, lad," Vetch remarked from above.

"If silence and gloom is what you want," put in one of the younger boys, "you could always try the Tower."

Ged said to him, "What is it you want, then, Jasper?"

"I want the company of my equals," Jasper said. "Come on, Vetch. Leave the prentices to their toys."

Ged turned to face Jasper. "What do sorcerers have that prentices lack?" he inquired. His voice was quiet, but all the other boys suddenly fell still, for in his tone as in Jasper's the spite between them now sounded plain and clear as steel coming out of a sheath.

"Power," Jasper said.

"I'll match your power act for act."

"You challenge me?"

"I challenge you."

Vetch had dropped down to the ground, and now he came between them, grim of face. "Duels in sorcery are forbidden to us, and well you know it. Let this cease!"

Both Ged and Jasper stood silent, for it was true they knew the law of Roke, and they also knew that Vetch was moved by love, and themselves by hate. Yet their anger was balked, not cooled. Presently, moving a little aside as if to be heard by Vetch alone, Jasper spoke, with his cool smile: "I think you'd better remind your goatherd friend again of the law that protects him. He looks sulky. I wonder, did he really think I'd accept a challenge from him? a fellow who smells of goats, a prentice who doesn't know the First Change?"

"Jasper," said Ged, "What do you know of what I know?"

For an instant, with no word spoken that any heard, Ged vanished from their sight, and where he had stood a great falcon hovered, opening its hooked beak to scream: for one instant, and then Ged stood again in the flickering torchlight, his dark gaze on Jasper.

Jasper had taken a step backward, in astonishment; but now he shrugged and said one word: "Illusion."

The others muttered. Vetch said, "That was not illusion. It was true change. And enough. Jasper, listen—"

"Enough to prove that he sneaked a look in the Book of Shaping behind the Master's back: what then? Go on, Goatherd. I like this trap you're building for yourself. The more you try to prove yourself my equal, the more you show yourself for what you are."

At that, Vetch turned from Jasper, and said very softly to Ged, "Sparrowhawk, will you be a man and drop this now—come with me—"

Ged looked at his friend and smiled, but all he said was, "Keep Hoeg for me a little while, will you?" He put into Vetch's hands the little otak, which as usual had been riding on his shoulder. It had never let any but Ged touch it, but it came to Vetch now, and climbing up his arm cowered on his shoulder, its great bright eyes always on its master.

"Now," Ged said to Jasper, quietly as before, "what are you going to do to prove yourself my superior, Jasper?"

"I don't have to do anything, Goatherd. Yet I will. I will give you a chance—an opportunity. Envy eats you like a worm in an apple. Let's let out the worm. Once by Roke Knoll you boasted that Gontish wizards don't play games. Come to Roke Knoll now and show us what it is they do instead. And afterward, maybe I will show you a little sorcery."

"Yes, I should like to see that," Ged answered. The younger boys, used to seeing his black temper break out at the least hint of slight or insult, watched him in wonder at his coolness now. Vetch watched him not in wonder, but with growing fear. He tried to intervene again, but Jasper said, "Come, keep out of this, Vetch. What will you do with the chance I give you, Goatherd? Will you show us an illusion, a fireball, a charm to cure goats with the mange?"

"What would you like me to do, Jasper?"

The older lad shrugged, "Summon up a spirit from the dead, for all I care!"

"I will."

"You will not." Jasper looked straight at him, rage suddenly flaming out over his disdain. "You will not. You cannot. You brag and brag—"

"By my name, I will do it!"

They all stood utterly motionless for a moment.

Breaking away from Vetch who would have held him back by main force, Ged strode out of the courtyard, not looking back. The dancing werelights overhead died out, sinking down. Jasper hesitated a second, then followed after Ged. And the rest came straggling behind, in silence, curious and afraid.

The slopes of Roke Knoll went up dark into the darkness of summer night before moonrise. The presence of that hill where many wonders had been worked was heavy, like a weight in the air about them. As they came onto the hillside they thought of how the roots of it were deep, deeper than the sea, reaching down even to the old, blind, secret fires at the world's core. They stopped on the east slope. Stars hung over the black grass above them on the hill's crest. No wind blew.

Ged went a few paces up the slope away from the others and turning said in a clear voice, "Jasper! Whose spirit shall I call?"

"Call whom you like. None will listen to you." Jasper's voice shook a little, with anger perhaps. Ged answered him softly, mockingly, "Are you afraid?"

He did not even listen for Jasper's reply, if he made one. He no longer cared about Jasper. Now that they stood on Roke Knoll, hate and rage were gone, replaced by utter certainty. He need envy no one. He knew that his power, this night, on this dark enchanted ground, was greater than it had ever been, filling him till he trembled with the sense of strength barely kept in check. He knew now that Jasper was far beneath him, had been sent perhaps only to bring him here tonight, no rival but a mere servant of Ged's destiny. Under his feet he felt the hillroots going down and down into the dark, and over his head he saw the dry, far fires of the stars. Between, all things were his to order, to command. He stood at the center of the world.

"Don't be afraid," he said, smiling. "I'll call a woman's spirit. You need not fear a woman. Elfarran I will call, the fair lady of the *Deed of Enlad*."

"She died a thousand years ago, her bones lie afar under the Sea of Éa, and maybe there never was such a woman."

"Do years and distances matter to the dead? Do the Songs lie?" Ged said with the same gentle mockery, and then saying, "Watch the air between my hands," he turned away from the others and stood still.

In a great slow gesture he stretched out his arms, the gesture of welcome that opens an invocation. He began to speak.

He had read the runes of this Spell of Summoning in Ogion's book, two years and more ago, and never since had seen them. In darkness he had read them then. Now in this darkness it was as if he read them again on the page open before him in the night. But now he understood what he read, speaking it aloud word after word, and he saw the markings of how the spell must be woven with the sound of the voice and the motion of body and hand.

The other boys stood watching, not speaking, not moving unless they shivered a little: for the great spell was beginning to work. Ged's voice was soft still, but changed, with a deep singing in it, and the words he spoke were not known to them. He fell silent. Suddenly the wind rose roaring in the grass. Ged dropped to his knees and called out aloud. Then he fell forward as if to embrace earth with his outstretched arms, and when he rose he held something dark in his straining hands and arms, something so heavy that he shook with effort getting to his feet. The hot wind whined in the black tossing grasses on the hill. If the stars shone now none saw them.

The words of the enchantment hissed and mumbled on Ged's lips, and then he cried out aloud and clearly, "Elfarran!"

Again he cried the name, "Elfarran!"

The shapeless mass of darkness he had lifted split apart. It sundered, and a pale spindle of light gleamed between his opened arms, a faint oval reaching from the ground up to the height of his raised hands. In the oval of light for a moment there moved a form, a human shape: a tall woman looking back over her shoulder. Her face was beautiful, and sorrowful, and full of fear.

Only for a moment did the spirit glimmer there. Then the sallow oval between Ged's arms grew bright. It widened and spread, a rent in the darkness of the earth and night, a ripping open of the fabric of the world. Through it blazed a terrible brightness. And through that bright misshapen breach clambered something like a clot of black shadow, quick and hideous, and it leaped straight out at Ged's face.

Staggering back under the weight of the thing, Ged gave a short, hoarse scream. The little otak watching from Vetch's shoulder, the animal that had no voice, screamed aloud also and leaped as if to attack.

Ged fell, struggling and writhing, while the bright rip in the world's darkness above him widened and stretched. The boys that watched fled, and Jasper bent down to the ground hiding his eyes from the terrible light. Vetch alone ran forward to his friend. So only he saw the lump of shadow that clung to Ged, tearing at his flesh. It was like a black beast, the size of a young child, though it seemed to swell and shrink; and it had no head or face, only the four taloned paws with which it gripped and tore. Vetch sobbed with horror, yet he put out his hands to try to pull the thing away from Ged. Before he touched it, he was bound still, unable to move.

The intolerable brightness faded, and slowly the torn edges of the world closed together. Nearby a

voice was speaking as softly as a tree whispers or a
fountain plays.

Starlight began to shine again, and the grasses of
the hillside were whitened with the light of the moon
just rising. The night was healed. Restored and
steady lay the balance of light and dark. The
shadow-beast was gone. Ged lay sprawled on his
back, his arms flung out as if they yet kept the wide
gesture of welcome and invocation. His face was
blackened with blood and there were great black
stains on his shirt. The little otak cowered by his
shoulder, quivering. And above him stood an old man
whose cloak glimmered pale in the moonrise: the
Archmage Nemmerle.

The end of Nemmerle's staff hovered silvery above
Ged's breast. Once gently it touched him over the
heart, once on the lips, while Nemmerle whispered.
Ged stirred, and his lips parted gasping for breath.
Then the old Archmage lifted the staff, and set it to
earth, and leaned heavily on it with bowed head, as if
he had scarcely strength to stand.

Vetch found himself free to move. Looking around,
he saw that already others were there, the Masters
Summoner and Changer. An act of great wizardry is
not worked without arousing such men, and they had
ways of coming very swiftly when need called,
though none had been so swift as the Archmage.
They now sent for help, and some who came went
with the Archmage, while others, Vetch among them,
carried Ged to the chambers of the Master Herbal.

All night long the Summoner stayed on Roke Knoll,
keeping watch. Nothing stirred there on the hillside
where the stuff of the world had been torn open. No
shadow came crawling through moonlight seeking the
rent through which it might clamber back into its
own domain. It had fled from Nemmerle, and from
the mighty spell-walls that surround and protect Roke

Island, but it was in the world now. In the world, somewhere, it hid. If Ged had died that night it might have tried to find the doorway he had opened, and follow him into death's realm, or slip back into whatever place it had come from; for this the Summoner waited on Roke Knoll. But Ged lived.

They had laid him abed in the healing-chamber, and the Master Herbal tended the wounds he had on his face and throat and shoulder. They were deep, ragged, and evil wounds. The black blood in them would not stanch, welling out even under the charms and the cobweb-wrapped perriot leaves laid upon them. Ged lay blind and dumb in fever like a stick in a slow fire, and there was no spell to cool what burned him.

Not far away, in the unroofed court where the fountain played, the Archmage lay also unmoving, but cold, very cold: only his eyes lived, watching the fall of moonlit water and the stir of moonlit leaves. Those with him said no spells and worked no healing. Quietly they spoke among themselves from time to time, and then turned again to watch their Lord. He lay still, hawk nose and high forehead and white hair bleached by moonlight all to the color of bone. To check the ungoverned spell and drive off the shadow from Ged, Nemmerle had spent all his power, and with it his bodily strength was gone. He lay dying. But the death of a great mage, who has many times in his life walked on the dry steep hillsides of death's kingdom, is a strange matter: for the dying man goes not blindly, but surely, knowing the way. When Nemmerle looked up through the leaves of the tree, those with him did not know if he watched the stars of summer fading in daybreak, or those other stars, which never set above the hills that see no dawn.

The raven of Osskil that had been his pet for thirty years was gone. No one had seen where it went. "It flies before him," the Master Patterner said, as they kept vigil.

The day came warm and clear. The Great House and the streets of Thwil were hushed. No voice was raised, until along towards noon iron bells spoke out aloud in the Chanter's Tower, harshly tolling.

On the next day the Nine Masters of Roke gathered in a place somewhere under the dark trees of the Immanent Grove. Even there they set nine walls of silence about them, that no person or power might speak to them or hear them as they chose from amongst the mages of all Earthsea him who would be the new Archmage. Gensher of Way was chosen. A ship was sent forth at once across the Inmost Sea to Way Island to bring the Archmage back to Roke. The Master Windkey stood in the stern and raised up the magewind into the sail, and quickly the ship departed, and was gone.

Of these events Ged knew nothing. For four weeks of that hot summer he lay blind, and deaf, and mute, though at times he moaned and cried out like an animal. At last, as the patient crafts of the Master Herbal worked their healing, his wounds began to close and the fever left him. Little by little he seemed to hear again, though he never spoke. On a clear day of autumn the Master Herbal opened the shutters of the room where Ged lay. Since the darkness of that night on Roke Knoll he had known only darkness. Now he saw daylight, and the sun shining. He hid his scarred face in his hands and wept.

Still when winter came he could speak only with a stammering tongue, and the Master Herbal kept him there in the healing-chambers, trying to lead his body and mind gradually back to strength. It was early spring when at last the Master released him, sending him first to offer his fealty to the Archmage Gensher. For he had not been able to join all the others of the School in this duty when Gensher came to Roke.

None of his companions had been allowed to visit him in the months of his sickness, and now as he passed some of them asked one another, "Who is that?"

He had been light and lithe and strong. Now, lamed by pain, he went hesitantly, and did not raise his face, the left side of which was white with scars. He avoided those who knew him and those who did not, and made his way straight to the court of the Fountain. There where once he had awaited Nemmerle, Gensher awaited him.

Like the old Archmage the new one was cloaked in white; but like most men of Way and the East Reach Gensher was black-skinned, and his look was black, under thick brows.

Ged knelt and offered him fealty and obedience. Gensher was silent a while.

"I know what you did," he said at last, "but not what you are. I cannot accept your fealty."

Ged stood up, and set his hand on the trunk of the young tree beside the fountain to steady himself. He was still very slow to find words. "Am I to leave Roke, my lord?"

"Do you want to leave Roke?"

"No."

"What do you want?"

"To stay. To learn. To undo ... the evil. ..."

"Nemmerle himself could not do that.—No, I would not let you go from Roke. Nothing protects you but the power of the Masters here and the defenses laid upon this island that keep the creatures of evil away. If you left now, the thing you loosed would find you at once, and enter into you, and possess you. You would be no man but a *gebbeth*, a puppet doing the will of that evil shadow which you raised up into the sunlight. You must stay here, until you gain strength and wisdom enough to defend yourself from it—if ever you do. Even now it waits for you. Assuredly it waits for you. Have you seen it since that night?"

"In dreams, lord." After a while Ged went on, speaking with pain and shame, "Lord Gensher, I do not know what it was—the thing that came out of the spell and cleaved to me—"

"Nor do I know. It has no name. You have great power inborn in you, and you used that power wrongly, to work a spell over which you had no control, not knowing how that spell affects the balance of light and dark, life and death, good and evil. And you were moved to do this by pride and by hate. Is it any wonder the result was ruin? You summoned a spirit from the dead, but with it came one of the Powers of unlife. Uncalled it came from a place where there are no names. Evil, it wills to work evil through you. The power you had to call it gives it power over you: you are connected. It is the shadow of your arrogance, the shadow of your ignorance, the shadow you cast. Has a shadow a name?"

Ged stood sick and haggard. He said at last, "Better I had died."

"Who are you to judge that, you for whom Nemmerle gave his life?—You are safe here. You will live here, and go on with your training. They tell me you were clever. Go on and do your work. Do it well. It is all you can do."

So Gensher ended, and was suddenly gone, as is the way of mages. The fountain leaped in the sunlight, and Ged watched it a while and listened to its voice, thinking of Nemmerle. Once in that court he had felt himself to be a word spoken by the sunlight. Now the darkness also had spoken: a word that could not be unsaid.

He left the court, going to his old room in the South Tower, which they had kept empty for him. He stayed there alone. When the gong called to supper he went, but he would hardly speak to the other lads at the Long Table, or raise his face to them, even those who greeted him most gently. So after a day or two they all left him alone. To be alone was his desire, for he feared the evil he might do or say unwittingly.

Neither Vetch nor Jasper was there, and he did not ask about them. The boys he had led and lorded over were all ahead of him now, because of the months he had lost, and that spring and summer he studied with lads younger than himself. Nor did he shine among them, for the words of any spell, even the simplest illusion-charm, came halting from his tongue, and his hands faltered at their craft.

In autumn he was to go once again to the Isolate Tower to study with the Master Namer. This task which he had once dreaded now pleased him, for silence was what he sought, and long learning where no spells were wrought, and where that power which he knew was still in him would never be called upon to act.

The night before he left for the Tower a visitor came to his room, one wearing a brown travelling-cloak and carrying a staff of oak shod with iron. Ged stood up, at sight of the wizard's staff.

"Sparrowhawk—"

At the sound of the voice, Ged raised his eyes: it was Vetch standing there, solid and foursquare as ever, his black blunt face older but his smile unchanged. On his shoulder crouched a little beast, brindle-furred and bright-eyed.

"He stayed with me while you were sick, and now I'm sorry to part with him. And sorrier to part with you, Sparrowhawk. But I'm going home. Here, hoeg! go to your true master!" Vetch patted the otak and set it down on the floor. It went and sat on Ged's pallet, and began to wash its fur with a dry brown tongue like a little leaf. Vetch laughed, but Ged could not smile. He bent down to hide his face, stroking the otak.

"I thought you wouldn't come to me, Vetch," he said.

He did not mean any reproach, but Vetch answered, "I couldn't come to you. The Master Herbal forbade me; and since winter I've been with the Master in the Grove, locked up myself. I was not free, until I earned my staff. Listen: when you too are free, come to the East Reach. I will be waiting for you. There's good cheer in the little towns there, and wizards are well received."

"Free ..." Ged muttered, and shrugged a little, trying to smile.

Vetch looked at him, not quite as he had used to look, with no less love but more wizardry, perhaps. He said gently, "You won't stay bound on Roke forever."

"Well ... I have thought, perhaps I may come to work with the Master in the Tower, to be one of those who seek among the books and the stars for lost names, and so ... so do no more harm, if not much good. ..."

"Maybe," said Vetch. "I am no seer, but I see before you, not rooms and books, but far seas, and the fire of dragons, and the towers of cities, and all such things a hawk sees when he flies far and high."

"And behind me—what do you see behind me?" Ged asked, and stood up as he spoke, so that the werelight that burned overhead between them sent his shadow back against the wall and floor. Then he turned his face aside and said, stammering, "But tell me where you will go, what you will do."

"I will go home, to see my brothers and the sister you have heard me speak of. I left her a little child and soon she'll be having her Naming—it's strange to think of! And so I'll find me a job of wizardry somewhere among the little isles. Oh, I would stay and talk with you, but I can't, my ship goes out tonight and the tide is turned already. Sparrowhawk, if ever your way lies East, come to me. And if ever you need me, send for me, call on me by my name: Estarriol."

At that Ged lifted his scarred face, meeting his friend's eyes.

"Estarriol," he said, "my name is Ged."

Then quietly they bade each other farewell, and Vetch turned and went down the stone hallway, and left Roke.

Ged stood still a while, like one who has received great news, and must enlarge his spirit to receive it. It was a great gift that Vetch had given him, the knowledge of his true name.

No one knows a man's true name but himself and his namer. He may choose at length to tell it to his brother, or his wife, or his friend, yet even those few will never use it where any third person may hear it. In front of other people they will, like other people, call him by his use-name, his nickname—such a name as Sparrowhawk, and Vetch, and Ogion which means "fir-cone". If plain men hide their true name from all but a few they love and trust utterly, so much more must wizardly men, being more dangerous, and more endangered. Who knows a man's name, holds that man's life in his keeping. Thus to Ged who had lost faith in himself, Vetch had given that gift only a friend can give, the proof of unshaken, unshakable trust.

Ged sat down on his pallet and let the globe of werelight die, giving off as it faded a faint whiff of marsh-gas. He petted the otak, which stretched comfortably and went to sleep on his knee as if it had never slept anywhere else. The Great House was silent. It came to Ged's mind that this was the eve of his own Passage, the day on which Ogion had given him his name. Four years were gone since then. He remembered the coldness of the mountain spring through which he had walked naked and unnamed. He fell to thinking of other bright pools in the River Ar, where he had used to swim; and of Ten Alders village under the great slanting forests of the mountain; of the shadows of morning across the dusty village street, the fire leaping under bellows-blast in the smith's smelting-pit on a winter afternoon, the witch's dark fragrant hut where the air was heavy with smoke and wreathing spells. He had not thought of these things for a long time. Now they came back to him, on this night he was seventeen years old. All the years and places of his brief broken life came within mind's reach and made a whole again. He knew once more, at last, after this long, bitter, wasted time, who he was and where he was.

But where he must go in the years to come, that he could not see; and he feared to see it.

Next morning he set out across the island, the otak riding on his shoulder as it had used to. This time it took him three days, not two, to walk to the Isolate Tower, and he was bone-weary when he came in sight of the Tower above the spitting, hissing seas of the northern cape. Inside, it was dark as he remembered, and cold as he remembered, and Kurremkarmerruk sat on his high seat writing down lists of names. He glanced at Ged and said without welcome, as if Ged had never been away, "Go to bed; tired is stupid. Tomorrow you may open the Book of the Undertakings of the Makers, learning the names therein."

At winter's end he returned to the Great House. He was made sorcerer then, and the Archmage Gensher accepted at that time his fealty. Thenceforth he studied the high arts and enchantments, passing beyond arts of illusion to the works of real magery, learning what he must know to earn his wizard's staff. The trouble he had had in speaking spells wore off over the months, and skill returned into his hands: yet he was never so quick to learn as he had been, having learned a long hard lesson from fear. Yet no ill portents or encounters followed on his working even of the Great Spells of Making and Shaping, which are most perilous. He came to wonder at times if the shadow he had loosed might have grown weak, or fled somehow out of the world, for it came no more into his dreams. But in his heart he knew such hope was folly.

From the Masters and from ancient lore-books Ged learned what he could about such beings as this shadow he had loosed; little was there to learn. No such creature was described or spoken of directly.

There were at best hints here and there in the old books of things that might be like the shadow-beast. It was not a ghost of human man, nor was it a creature of the Old Powers of Earth, and yet it seemed it might have some link with these. In the *Matter of the Dragons*, which Ged read very closely, there was a tale of an ancient Dragonlord who had come under the sway of one of the Old Powers, a speaking stone that lay in a far northern land. *"At the Stone's command,"* said the book, *"he did speak to raise up a dead spirit out of the realm of the dead, but his wizardry being bent awry by the Stone's will there came with the dead spirit also a thing not summoned, which did devour him out from within and in his shape walked, destroying men."* But the book did not say what the thing was, nor did it tell the end of the tale. And the Masters did not know where such a shadow might come from: from unlife, the Archmage had said; from the wrong side of the world, said the Master Changer; and the Master Summoner said, "I do not know." The Summoner had come often to sit with Ged in his illness. He was grim and grave as ever, but Ged knew now his compassion, and loved him well. "I do not know. I know of the thing only this: that only a great power could have summoned up such a thing, and perhaps only one power—only one voice—your voice. But what in turn that means, I do not know. You will find out. You must find out, or die, and worse than die...." He spoke softly and his eyes were somber as he looked at Ged. "You thought, as a boy, that a mage is one who can do anything. So I thought, once. So did we all. And the truth is that as a man's real power grows and his knowledge widens, ever the way he can follow grows narrower: until at last he chooses nothing, but does only and wholly what he *must do*...."

The Archmage sent Ged, after his eighteenth birthday, to work with the Master Patterner. What is learned in the Immanent Grove is not much talked about elsewhere. It is said that no spells are worked there, and yet the place itself is an enchantment. Sometimes the trees of that Grove are seen, and sometimes they are not seen, and they are not always in the same place and part of Roke Island. It is said that the trees of the Grove themselves are wise. It is said that the Master Patterner learns his supreme magery there within the Grove, and if ever the trees should die so shall his wisdom die, and in those days the waters will rise and drown the islands of Earthsea which Segoy raised from the deeps in the time before myth, all the lands where men and dragons dwell.

But all this is hearsay; wizards will not speak of it.

The months went by, and at last on a day of spring Ged returned to the Great House, and he had no idea what would be asked of him next. At the door that gives on the path across the fields to Roke Knoll an old man met him, waiting for him in the doorway. At first Ged did not know him, and then putting his mind to it recalled him as the one who had let him into the School on the day of his coming, five years ago.

The old man smiled, greeting him by name, and asked, "Do you know who I am?"

Now Ged had thought before of how it was always said, the Nine Masters of Roke, although he knew only eight: Windkey, Hand, Herbal, Chanter, Changer, Summoner, Namer, Patterner. It seemed that people spoke of the Archmage as the ninth. Yet when a new Archmage was chosen, nine Masters met to choose him.

"I think you are the Master Doorkeeper," said Ged.

"I am. Ged, you won entrance to Roke by saying your name. Now you may win your freedom of it by saying mine." So said the old man smiling, and waited. Ged stood dumb.

He knew a thousand ways and crafts and means for finding out names of things and of men, of course; such craft was a part of everything he had learned at

Roke, for without it there could be little useful magic done. But to find out the name of a Mage and Master was another matter. A mage's name is better hidden than a herring in the sea, better guarded than a dragon's den. A prying charm will be met with a stronger charm, subtle devices will fail, devious inquiries will be deviously thwarted, and force will be turned ruinously back upon itself.

"You keep a narrow door, Master," said Ged at last. "I must sit out in the fields here, I think, and fast till I grow thin enough to slip through."

"As long as you like," said the Doorkeeper, smiling.

So Ged went off a little way and sat down under an alder on the banks of the Thwilburn, letting his otak run down to play in the stream and hunt the muddy banks for creek-crabs. The sun went down, late and bright, for spring was well along. Lights of lantern and werelight gleamed in the windows of the Great House, and down the hill the streets of Thwil town filled with darkness. Owls hooted over the roofs and bats flitted in the dusk air above the stream, and still Ged sat thinking how he might, by force, ruse, or sorcery, learn the Doorkeeper's name. The more he pondered the less he saw, among all the arts of witchcraft he had learned in these five years on Roke, any one that would serve to wrest such a secret from such a mage.

He lay down in the field and slept under the stars, with the otak nestling in his pocket. After the sun was up he went, still fasting, to the door of the House and knocked. The Doorkeeper opened.

"Master," said Ged, "I cannot take your name from you, not being strong enough, and I cannot trick your name from you, not being wise enough. So I am content to stay here, and learn or serve, whatever you will: unless by chance you will answer a question I have."

"Ask it."

"What is your name?"

The Doorkeeper smiled, and said his name: and Ged, repeating it, entered for the last time into that House.

When he left it again he wore a heavy dark-blue cloak, the gift of the township of Low Torning, whereto he was bound, for they wanted a wizard there. He carried also a staff of his own height, carved of yew-wood, bronze-shod. The Doorkeeper bade him farewell opening the back door of the Great House for him, the door of horn and ivory, and he went down the streets of Thwil to a ship that waited for him on the bright water in the morning.

# 5 The Dragon of Pendor

West of Roke in a crowd between the two great lands Hosk and Ensmer lie the Ninety Isles. The nearest to Roke is Serd, and the farthest is Seppish, which lies almost in the Pelnish Sea; and whether the sum of them is ninety is a question never settled, for if you count only isles with freshwater springs you might have seventy, while if you count every rock you might have a hundred and still not be done; and then the tide would change. Narrow run the channels between the islets, and there the mild tides of the Inmost Sea, chafed and baffled, run high and fall low, so that where at high tide there might be three islands in one place, at low there might be one. Yet for all that danger of the tide, every child who can walk can paddle, and has his little rowboat; housewives row across the channel to take a cup of rushwash tea with the neighbor; peddlers call their wares in rhythm with the stroke of their oars. All roads there are salt water, blocked only by nets strung from house to house across the straits to catch the small

75

fish called turbies, the oil of which is the wealth of
the Ninety Isles. There are few bridges, and no great
towns. Every islet is thick with farms and fishermen's
houses, and these are gathered into townships each of
ten or twenty islets. One such was Low Torning, the
westernmost, looking not on the Inmost Sea but outward to empty ocean, that lonely corner of the
Archipelago where only Pendor lies, the dragon-
spoiled isle, and beyond it the waters of the West
Reach, desolate.

A house was ready there for the township's new
wizard. It stood on a hill among green fields of bar-
ley, sheltered from the west wind by a grove of pendick-trees that now were red with flowers. From the
door one looked out on other thatched roofs and groves
and gardens, and other islands with their roofs and
fields and hills, and amongst them all the many
bright winding channels of the sea. It was a poor
house, windowless, with earthen floor, yet a better
house than the one Ged was born in. The Isle-Men of
Low Torning, standing in awe of the wizard from
Roke, asked pardon for its humbleness. "We have no
stone to build with," said one, "We are none of us
rich, though none starve," said another, and a third,
"It will be dry at least, for I saw to the thatching myself, Sir." To Ged it was as good as any palace. He
thanked the leaders of the township frankly, so that
the eighteen of them went home, each in his own
rowboat to his home isle, to tell the fishermen and
housewives that the new wizard was a strange young
grim fellow who spoke little, but he spoke fairly, and
without pride.

There was little cause, perhaps, for pride in this
first magistry of Ged's. Wizards trained on Roke went
commonly to cities or castles, to serve high lords who
held them in high honor. These fisherman of Low
Torning in the usual way of things would have had
among them no more than a witch or a plain sorcerer,
to charm the fishing-nets and sing over new boats and

cure beasts and men of their ailments. But in late
years the old Dragon of Pendor had spawned: nine
dragons, it was said, now laired in the ruined towers
of the Sealords of Pendor, dragging their scaled bel-
lies up and down the marble stairs and through the
broken doorways there. Wanting food on that dead
isle, they would be flying forth some year when they
were grown and hunger came upon them. Already a
flight of four had been seen over the southwest shores
of Hosk, not alighting but spying out the sheepfolds,
barns, and villages. The hunger of a dragon is slow to
wake, but hard to sate. So the Isle-Men of Low Torning had sent to Roke begging for a wizard to protect
their folk from what boded over the western horizon,
and the Archmage had judged their fear well founded.

"There is no comfort in this place," the Archmage
had said to Ged on the day he made him wizard, "no
fame, no wealth, maybe no risk. Will you go?"

"I will go," Ged had replied, not from obedience
only. Since the night on Roke Knoll his desire had
turned as much against fame and display as once it
had been set on them. Always now he doubted his
strength and dreaded the trial of his power. Yet also
the talk of dragons drew him with a great curiosity.
In Gont there have been no dragons for many hundred years; and no dragon would ever fly within
scent or sight or spell of Roke, so that there also they
are a matter of tales and songs only, things sung of
but not seen. Ged had learned all he could of dragons
at the School, but it is one thing to read about
dragons and another to meet them. The chance lay
bright before him, and heartily he answered, "I will
go."

The Archmage Gensher had nodded his head, but
his look was somber. "Tell me," he said at last, "do
you fear to leave Roke? or are you eager to be gone?"

"Both, my lord."

Again Gensher nodded. "I do not know if I do right
to send you from your safety here," he said very low.

"I cannot see your way. It is all in darkness. And there is a power in the North, something that would destroy you, but what it is and where, whether in your past or on your forward way, I cannot tell: it is all shadowed. When the men from Low Torning came here, I thought at once of you, for it seemed a safe place and out of the way, where you might have time to gather your strength. But I do not know if any place is safe for you, or where your way goes. I do not want to send you out into the dark...."

It seemed a bright enough place to Ged at first, the house under the flowering trees. There he lived, and watched the western sky often, and kept his wizard's ear tuned for the sound of scaly wings. But no dragon came. Ged fished from his jetty, and tended his garden-patch. He spent whole days pondering a page or a line or a word in the Lore-Books he had brought from Roke, sitting out in the summer air under the pendick-trees, while the otak slept beside him or went hunting mice in the forests of grass and daisies. And he served the people of Low Torning as healall and weatherworker whenever they asked him. It did not enter his head that a wizard might be ashamed to perform such simple crafts, for he had been a witch-child among poorer folk than these. They, however, asked little of him, holding him in awe, partly because he was a wizard from the Isle of the Wise, and partly on account of his silence and his scarred face. There was that about him, young as he was, that made men uneasy with him.

Yet he found a friend, a boatmaker who dwelt on the next islet eastward. His name was Pechvarry. They had met first on his jetty, where Ged stopped to watch him stepping the mast of a little catboat. He had looked up at the wizard with a grin and said, "Here's a month's work nearly finished. I guess you might have done it in a minute with a word, eh, Sir?"

"I might," said Ged, "but it would likely sink the

next minute, unless I kept the spells up. But if you like . . ." He stopped.

"Well, Sir?"

"Well, that is a lovely little craft. She needs nothing. But if you like, I could set a binding-spell on her, to help keep her sound; or a finding-spell, to help bring her home from the sea."

He spoke hesitantly, not wanting to offend the craftsman, but Pechvarry's face shone. "The little boat's for my son, Sir, and if you would lay such charms on her, it would be a mighty kindness and a friendly act." And he climbed up onto the jetty to take Ged's hand then and there and thank him.

After that they came to work together often, Ged interweaving his spellcrafts with Pechvarry's handwork on the boats he built or repaired, and in return learning from Pechvarry how a boat was built, and also how a boat was handled without aid of magic: for this skill of plain sailing had been somewhat scanted on Roke. Often Ged and Pechvarry and his little son Ioeth went out into the channels and lagoons, sailing or rowing one boat or another, till Ged was a fair sailor, and the friendship between him and Pechvarry was a settled thing.

Along in late autumn the boatmaker's son fell sick. The mother sent for the witchwoman of Tesk Isle, who was a good hand at healing, and all seemed well for a day or two. Then in the middle of a stormy night came Pechvarry hammering at Ged's door, begging him to come save the child. Ged ran down to the boat with him and they rowed in all haste through dark and rain to the boatmaker's house. There Ged saw the child on his pallet-bed, and the mother crouching silent beside him, and the witchwoman making a smoke of corly-root and singing the Nagian Chant, which was the best healing she had. But she whispered to Ged, "Lord Wizard, I think this fever is the redfever, and the child will die of it tonight."

When Ged knelt and put his hands on the child, he

thought the same, and he drew back a moment. In the latter months of his own long sickness the Master Herbal had taught him much of the healer's lore, and the first lesson and the last of all that lore was this: Heal the wound and cure the illness, but let the dying spirit go.

The mother saw his movement and the meaning of it, and cried out aloud in despair. Pechvarry stooped down by her saying, "The Lord Sparrowhawk will save him, wife. No need to cry! He's here now. He can do it."

Hearing the mother's wail, and seeing the trust Pechvarry had in him, Ged did not know how he could disappoint them. He mistrusted his own judgment, and thought perhaps the child might be saved, if the fever could be brought down. He said, "I'll do my best, Pechvarry."

He set to bathing the little boy with cold rainwater that they brought new-fallen from out of doors, and he began to say one of the spells of feverstay. The spell took no hold and made no whole, and suddenly he thought the child was dying in his arms.

Summoning his power all at once and with no thought for himself, he sent his spirit out after the child's spirit, to bring it back home. He called the child's name, "Ioeth!" Thinking some faint answer came in his inward hearing he pursued, calling once more. Then he saw the little boy running fast and far ahead of him down a dark slope, the side of some vast hill. There was no sound. The stars above the hill were no stars his eyes had ever seen. Yet he knew the constellations by name: the Sheaf, the Door, the One Who Turns, the Tree. They were those stars that do not set, that are not paled by the coming of any day. He had followed the dying child too far.

Knowing this he found himself alone on the dark hillside. It was hard to turn back, very hard.

He turned slowly. Slowly he set one foot forward to climb back up the hill, and then the other. Step by step he went, each step willed. And each step was harder than the last.

The stars did not move. No wind blew over the dry steep ground. In all the vast kingdom of the darkness only he moved, slowly, climbing. He came to the top of the hill, and saw the low wall of stones there. But across the wall, facing him, there was a shadow.

The shadow did not have the shape of man or beast. It was shapeless, scarcely to be seen, but it whispered at him, though there were no words in its whispering, and it reached out towards him. And it stood on the side of the living, and he on the side of the dead.

Either he must go down the hill into the desert lands and lightless cities of the dead, or he must step across the wall back into life, where the formless evil thing waited for him.

His spirit-staff was in his hand, and he raised it high. With that motion, strength came into him. As he made to leap the low wall of stones straight at the shadow, the staff burned suddenly white, a blinding light in that dim place. He leaped, felt himself fall, and saw no more.

Now what Pechvarry and his wife and the witch saw was this: the young wizard had stopped midway in his spell, and held the child a while motionless. Then he had laid little Ioeth gently down on the pallet, and had risen, and stood silent, staff in hand. All at once he raised the staff high and it blazed with white fire as if he held the lightning-bolt in his grip, and all the household things in the hut leaped out strange and vivid in that momentary fire. When their eyes were clear from the dazzlement they saw the young man lying huddled forward on the earthen floor, beside the pallet where the child lay dead.

To Pechvarry it seemed that the wizard also was dead. His wife wept, but he was utterly bewildered. But the witch had some hearsay knowledge concerning magery and the ways a true wizard may go, and

she saw to it that Ged, cold and lifeless as he lay, was
not treated as a dead man but as one sick or tranced.
He was carried home, and an old woman was left to
watch and see whether he slept to wake or slept for
ever.

The little otak was hiding in the rafters of the
house, as it did when strangers entered. There it
stayed while the rain beat on the walls and the fire
sank down and the night wearing slowly along left
the old woman nodding beside the hearthpit. Then
the otak crept down and came to Ged where he lay
stretched stiff and still upon the bed. It began to lick
his hands and wrists, long and patiently, with its dry
leaf-brown tongue. Crouching beside his head it
licked his temple, his scarred cheek, and softly his
closed eyes. And very slowly under that soft touch
Ged roused. He woke, not knowing where he had
been or where he was or what was the faint grey
light in the air about him, which was the light of
dawn coming to the world. Then the otak curled up
near his shoulder as usual, and went to sleep.

Later, when Ged thought back upon that night, he
knew that had none touched him when he lay thus
spirit-lost, had none called him back in some way, he
might have been lost for good. It was only the dumb
instinctive wisdom of the beast who licks his hurt
companion to comfort him, and yet in that wisdom
Ged saw something akin to his own power, something
that went as deep as wizardry. From that time forth
he believed that the wise man is one who never sets
himself apart from other living things, whether they
have speech or not, and in later years he strove long
to learn what can be learned, in silence, from the
eyes of animals, the flight of birds, the great slow gestures of trees.

He had now made unscathed, for the first time,
that crossing-over and return which only a wizard
can make with open eyes, and which not the greatest
mage can make without risk. But he had returned to

a grief and a fear. The grief was for his friend Pechvarry, the fear was for himself. He knew now why the Archmage had feared to send him forth, and what had darkened and clouded even the mage's forseeing of his future. For it was darkness itself that had awaited him, the unnamed thing, the being that did not belong in the world, the shadow he had loosed or made. In spirit, at the boundary wall between death and life, it had waited for him these long years. It had found him there at last. It would be on his track now, seeking to draw near to him, to take his strength into itself, and suck up his life, and clothe itself in his flesh.

Soon after, he dreamed of the thing like a bear with no head or face. He thought it went fumbling about the walls of the house, searching for the door. Such a dream he had not dreamed since the healing of the wounds the thing had given him. When he woke he was weak and cold, and the scars on his face and shoulder drew and ached.

Now began a bad time. When he dreamed of the shadow or so much as thought of it, he felt always that same cold dread: sense and power drained out of him, leaving him stupid and astray. He raged at his cowardice, but that did no good. He sought for some protection, but there was none: the thing was not flesh, not alive, not spirit, unnamed, having no being but what he himself had given it—a terrible power outside the laws of the sunlit world. All he knew of it was that it was drawn to him and would try to work its will through him, being his creature. But in what form it could come, having no real form of its own as yet, and how it would come, and when it would come, this he did not know.

He set up what barriers of sorcery he could about his house and about the isle where he lived. Such spell-walls must be ever renewed, and soon he saw that if he spent all his strength on these defenses, he would be of no use to the islanders. What could he do, between two enemies, if a dragon came from Pendor?

Again he dreamed, but this time in the dream the shadow was inside his house, beside the door, reaching out to him through the darkness and whispering words he did not understand. He woke in terror, and sent the werelight flaming through the air, lighting every corner of the little house till he saw no shadow anywhere. Then he put wood on the coals of his firepit, and sat in the firelight hearing the autumn wind fingering at the thatch roof and whining in the great bare trees above; and he pondered long. An old anger had awakened in his heart. He would not suffer this helpless waiting, this sitting trapped on a little island muttering useless spells of lock and ward. Yet he could not simply flee the trap: to do so would be to break his trust with the islanders and to leave them to the imminent dragon, undefended. There was but one way to take.

The next morning he went down among the fishermen in the principal moorage of Low Torning, and finding the Head Isle-Man there said to him, "I must leave this place. I am in danger, and I put you in danger. I must go. Therefore I ask your leave to go out and do away with the dragons on Pendor, so that my task for you will be finished and I may leave freely. Or if I fail, I should fail also when they come here, and that is better known now than later."

The Isle-Man stared at him all dropjawed. "Lord Sparrowhawk," he said, "there are nine dragons out there!"

"Eight are still young, they say."

"But the old one—"

"I tell you, I must go from here. I ask your leave to rid you of the dragon-peril first, if I can do so."

"As you will, Sir," the Isle-Man said gloomily. All that listened there thought this a folly or a crazy courage in their young wizard, and with sullen faces they saw him go, expecting no news of him again.

Some hinted that he meant merely to sail back by Hosk to the Inmost Sea, leaving them in the lurch; others, among them Pechvarry, held that he had gone mad, and sought death.

For four generations of men all ships had set their course to keep far from the shores of Pendor Island. No mage had ever come to do combat with the dragon there, for the island was on no travelled sea road, and its lords had been pirates, slave-takers, war-makers, hated by all that dwelt in the southwest parts of Earthsea. For this reason none had sought to revenge the Lord of Pendor, after the dragon came suddenly out of the west upon him and his men where they sat feasting in the tower, and smothered them with the flames of his mouth, and drove all the townsfolk screaming into the sea. Unavenged, Pendor had been left to the dragon, with all its bones, and towers, and jewels stolen from long-dead princes of the coasts of Paln and Hosk.

All this Ged knew well, and more, for ever since he came to Low Torning he had held in mind and pondered over all he had ever learned of dragons. As he guided his small boat westward—not rowing now nor using the seaman's skill Pechvarry had taught him, but sailing wizardly with the magewind in his sail and a spell set on prow and keel to keep them true—he watched to see the dead isle rise on the rim of the sea. Speed he wanted, and therefore used the magewind, for he feared what was behind him more than what was before him. But as the day passed, his impatience turned from fear to a kind of glad fierceness. At least he sought this danger of his own will; and the nearer he came to it the more sure he was that, for this time at least, for this hour perhaps before his death, he was free. The shadow dared not follow him into a dragon's jaws. The waves ran white-tipped on the grey sea, and grey clouds streamed overhead on the north wind. He went west with the quick magewind in his sail, and came in sight of the rocks of

Pendor, the still streets of the town, and the gutted, falling towers.

At the entrance of the harbor, a shallow crescent bay, he let the windspell drop and stilled his little boat so it lay rocking on the waves. Then he summoned the dragon: "Usurper of Pendor, come defend your hoard!"

His voice fell short in the sound of breakers beating on the ashen shores; but dragons have keen ears. Presently one flitted up from some roofless ruin of the town like a vast black bat, thin-winged and spiny-backed, and circling into the north wind came flying towards Ged. His heart swelled at the sight of the creature that was a myth to his people, and he laughed and shouted, "Go tell the Old One to come, you wind-worm!"

For this was one of the young dragons, spawned there years ago by a she-dragon from the West Reach, who had set her clutch of great leathern eggs, as they say she-dragons will, in some sunny broken room of the tower and had flown away again, leaving the Old Dragon of Pendor to watch the young when they crawled like baneful lizards from the shell.

The young dragon made no answer. He was not large of his kind, maybe the length of a forty-oared ship, and was worm-thin for all the reach of his black membranous wings. He had not got his growth yet, nor his voice, nor any dragon-cunning. Straight at Ged in the small rocking boat he came, opening his long, toothed jaws as he slid down arrowy from the air: so that all Ged had to do was bind his wings and limbs stiff with one sharp spell and send him thus hurtling aside into the sea like a stone falling. And the grey sea closed over him.

Two dragons like the first rose up from the base of the highest tower. Even as the first one they came driving straight at Ged, and even so he caught both, hurled both down, and drowned them; and he had not yet lifted up his wizard's staff.

Now after a little time there came three against him from the island. One of these was much greater, and fire spewed curling from its jaws. Two came flying at him rattling their wings, but the big one came circling from behind, very swift, to burn him and his boat with its breath of fire. No binding spell would catch all three, because two came from north and one from south. In the instant that he saw this, Ged worked a spell of Changing, and between one breath and the next flew up from his boat in dragon-form.

Spreading broad wings and reaching talons out, he met the two head on, withering them with fire, and then turned to the third, who was larger than he and armed also with fire. On the wind over the grey waves they doubled, snapped, swooped, lunged, till smoke roiled about them red-lit by the glare of their fiery mouths. Ged flew suddenly upward and the other pursued, below him. In midflight the dragon Ged raised wings, stopped, and stooped as the hawk stoops, talons outstretched downward, striking and bearing the other down by neck and flank. The black wings flurried and black dragon-blood dropped in thick drops into the sea. The Pendor dragon tore free and flew low and lamely to the island, where it hid, crawling into some well or cavern in the ruined town.

At once Ged took his form and place again on the boat, for it was most perilous to keep that dragon-shape longer than need demanded. His hands were black with the scalding wormblood, and he was scorched about the head with fire, but this was no matter now. He waited only till he had his breath back and then called, "Six I have seen, five slain, nine are told of: come out, worms!"

No creature moved nor voice spoke for a long while on the island, but only the waves beat loudly on the shore. Then Ged was aware that the highest tower slowly changed its shape, bulging out on one side as if it grew an arm. He feared dragon-magic, for old dragons are very powerful and guileful in a sorcery like and unlike the sorcery of men: but a moment more and he saw this was no trick of the dragon, but of his own eyes. What he had taken for a part of the tower was the shoulder of the Dragon of Pendor as he uncurled his bulk and lifted himself slowly up.

When he was all afoot his scaled head, spike-crowned and triple-tongued, rose higher than the broken tower's height, and his taloned forefeet rested on the rubble of the town below. His scales were grey-black, catching the daylight like broken stone. Lean as a hound he was and huge as a hill. Ged stared in awe. There was no song or tale could prepare the mind for this sight. Almost he stared into the dragon's eyes and was caught, for one cannot look into a dragon's eyes. He glanced away from the oily green gaze that watched him, and held up before him his staff, that looked now like a splinter, like a twig.

"Eight sons I had, little wizard," said the great dry voice of the dragon. "Five died, one dies: enough. You will not win my hoard by killing them."

"I do not want your hoard."

The yellow smoke hissed from the dragon's nostrils: that was his laughter.

"Would you not like to come ashore and look at it, little wizard? It is worth looking at."

"No, dragon." The kinship of dragons is with wind and fire, and they do not fight willingly over the sea. That had been Ged's advantage so far and he kept it; but the strip of seawater between him and the great grey talons did not seem much of an advantage, any more.

It was hard not to look into the green, watching eyes.

"You are a very young wizard," the dragon said, "I did not know men came so young into their power." He spoke, as did Ged, in the Old Speech, for that is the tongue of dragons still. Although the use of the

Old Speech binds a man to truth, this is not so with dragons. It is their own language, and they can lie in it, twisting the true words to false ends, catching the unwary hearer in a maze of mirrorwords each of which reflects the truth and none of which leads anywhere. So Ged had been warned often, and when the dragon spoke he listened with an untrustful ear, all his doubts ready. But the words seemed plain and clear: "Is it to ask my help that you have come here, little wizard?"

"No, dragon."

"Yet I could help you. You will need help soon, against that which hunts you in the dark."

Ged stood dumb.

"What is it that hunts you? Name it to me."

"If I could name it—" Ged stopped himself.

Yellow smoke curled above the dragon's long head, from the nostrils that were two round pits of fire.

"If you could name it you could master it, maybe, little wizard. Maybe I could tell you its name, when I see it close by. And it will come close, if you wait about my isle. It will come wherever you come. If you do not want it to come close you must run, and run, and keep running from it. And yet it will follow you. Would you like to know its name?"

Ged stood silent again. How the dragon knew of the shadow he had loosed, he could not guess, nor how it might know the shadow's name. The Archmage had said that the shadow had no name. Yet dragons have their own wisdom; and they are an older race than man. Few men can guess what a dragon knows and how he knows it, and those few are the Dragonlords. To Ged, only one thing was sure: that, though the dragon might well be speaking truth, though he might indeed be able to tell Ged the nature and name of the shadow-thing and so give him power over it—even so, even if he spoke truth, he did so wholly for his own ends.

"It is very seldom," the young man said at last, "that dragons ask to do men favors."

"But it is very common," said the dragon, "for cats to play with mice before they kill them."

"But I did not come here to play, or to be played with. I came to strike a bargain with you."

Like a sword in sharpness but five times the length of any sword, the point of the dragon's tail arched up scorpion-wise over his mailed back, above the tower. Dryly he spoke: "I strike no bargains. I take. What have you to offer that I cannot take from you when I like?"

"Safety. Your safety. Swear that you will never fly eastward of Pendor, and I will swear to leave you unharmed."

A grating sound came from the dragon's throat like the noise of an avalanche far off, stones falling among mountains. Fire danced along his three-forked tongue. He raised himself up higher, looming over the ruins. "You offer me safety! You threaten me! With what?"

"With your name, Yevaud."

Ged's voice shook as he spoke the name, yet he spoke it clear and loud. At the sound of it, the old dragon held still, utterly still. A minute went by, and another; and then Ged, standing there in his rocking chip of a boat, smiled. He had staked this venture and his life on a guess drawn from old histories of dragon-lore learned on Roke, a guess that this Dragon of Pendor was the same that had spoiled the west of Osskil in the days of Elfarran and Morred, and had been driven from Osskill by a wizard, Elt, wise in names. The guess had held.

"We are matched, Yevaud. You have the strength: I have your name. Will you bargain?"

Still the dragon made no reply.

Many years had the dragon sprawled on the island where golden breastplates and emeralds lay scattered among dust and bricks and bones; he had watched

his black lizard-brood play among crumbling houses
and try their wings from the cliffs; he had slept long
in the sun, unwaked by voice or sail. He had grown
old. It was hard now to stir, to face this mage-lad,
this frail enemy, at the sight of whose staff Yevaud,
the old dragon, winced.

"You may choose nine stones from my hoard," he
said at last, his voice hissing and whining in his long
jaws. "The best: take your choice. Then go!"

"I do not want your stones, Yevaud."

"Where is men's greed gone? Men loved bright
stones in the old days in the North. . . . I know what
it is you want, wizard. I, too, can offer you safety, for
I know what can save you. I know what alone can
save you. There is a horror follows you. I will tell you
its name."

Ged's heart leaped in him, and he clutched his
staff, standing as still as the dragon stood. He fought
a moment with sudden, startling hope.

It was not his own life that he bargained for. One
mastery, and only one, could he hold over the dragon.
He set hope aside and did what he must do.

"That is not what I ask for, Yevaud."

When he spoke the dragon's name it was as if he
held the huge being on a fine, thin leash, tightening it
on his throat. He could feel the ancient malice and
experience of men in the dragon's gaze that rested on
him, he could see the steel talons each as long as a
man's forearm, and the stone-hard hide, and the withering fire that lurked in the dragon's throat: and yet
always the leash tightened, tightened.

He spoke again: "Yevaud! Swear by your name
that you and your sons will never come to the
Archipelago."

Flames broke suddenly bright and loud from the
dragon's jaws, and he said, "I swear it by my name!"

Silence lay over the isle then, and Yevaud lowered
his great head.

When he raised it again and looked, the wizard

was gone, and the sail of the boat was a white fleck
on the waves eastward, heading towards the fat be-
jewelled islands of the inner seas. Then in rage the
old Dragon of Pendor rose up breaking the tower
with the writhing of his body, and beating his wings
that spanned the whole width of the ruined town. But
his oath held him, and he did not fly, then or ever, to
the Archipelago.

# 6 Hunted

As soon as Pendor had sunk under the sea-rim behind
him, Ged looking eastward felt the fear of the
shadow come into his heart again; and it was hard to
turn from the bright danger of the dragons to that
formless, hopeless horror. He let the magewind drop,
and sailed on with the world's wind, for there was no
desire for speed in him now. He had no clear plan
even of what he should do. He must run, as the
dragon had said; but where? To Roke, he thought,
since there at least he was protected, and might find
counsel among the wise.

First, however, he must come to Low Torning once
more and tell his tale to the Isle-Men. When word
went out that he had returned, five days from his setting forth, they and half the people of the township
came rowing and running to gather round him, and
stare at him, and listen. He told his tale, and one man
said, "But who saw this wonder of dragons slain and
dragons baffled? What if he—"

"Be still!" the Head Isle-Man said roughly, for he

knew, as did most of them, that a wizard may have subtle ways of telling the truth, and may keep the truth to himself, but that if he says a thing the thing is as he says. For that is his mastery. So they wondered, and began to feel that their fear was lifted from them, and then they began to rejoice. They pressed round their young wizard and asked for the tale again. More islanders came, and asked for it again. By nightfall he no longer had to tell it. They could do it for him, better. Already the village chanters had fitted it to an old tune, and were singing the *Song of the Sparrowhawk.* Bonfires were burning not only on the isles of Low Torning but in townships to the south and east. Fishermen shouted the news from boat to boat, from isle to isle it went: Evil is averted, the dragons will never come from Pendor!

That night, that one night, was joyous for Ged. No shadow could come near him through the brightness of those fires of thanksgiving that burned on every hill and beach, through the circles of laughing dancers that ringed him about, singing his praise, swinging their torches in the gusty autumn night so that sparks rose thick and bright and brief upon the wind.

The next day he met with Pechvarry, who said, "I did not know you were so mighty, my lord." There was fear in that because he had dared make Ged his friend, but there was reproach in it also. Ged had not saved a little child, though he had slain dragons. After that, Ged felt afresh the unease and impatience that had driven him to Pendor, and drove him now from Low Torning. The next day, though they would have kept him gladly the rest of his life to praise and boast of, he left the house on the hill, with no baggage but his books, his staff, and the otak riding on his shoulder.

He went in a rowboat with a couple of young fishermen of Low Torning, who wanted the honor of being his boatmen. Always as they rowed on among

the craft that crowd the eastern channels of the
Ninety Isles, under the windows and balconies of
houses that lean out over the water, past the wharves
of Nesh, the rainy pastures of Dromgan, the malodor-
ous oil-sheds of Geath, word of his deed had gone
ahead of him. They whistled the *Song of the Sparrowhawk* as he went by, they vied to have him spend
the night and tell his dragon-tale. When at last he
came to Serd, the ship's master of whom he asked
passage out to Roke bowed as he answered, "A privi-
lege to me, Lord Wizard, and an honor to my ship!"

So Ged turned his back on the Ninety Isles; but
even as the ship turned from Serd Inner Port and
raised sail, a wind came up hard from the east
against her. It was strange, for the wintry sky was
clear and the weather had seemed settled mild that
morning. It was only thirty miles from Serd to Roke,
and they sailed on; and when the wind still rose, they
still sailed on. The little ship, like most traders of the
Inmost Sea, bore the high fore-and-aft sail that can
be turned to catch a headwind, and her master was a
handy seaman, proud of his skill. So tacking now
north now south they worked eastward. Clouds and
rain came up on the wind, which veered and gusted
so wildly that there was considerable danger of the
ship jibing. "Lord Sparrowhawk," said the ship's master to the young man, whom he had beside him in the
place of honor in the stern, though small dignity
could be kept up under that wind and rain that wet
them all to a miserable sleekness in their sodden
cloaks—"Lord Sparrowhawk, might you say a word to
this wind, maybe?"

"How near are we to Roke?"

"Better than half way. But we've made no headway
at all this past hour, Sir."

Ged spoke to the wind. It blew less hard, and for a
while they went on fairly enough. Then sudden great
gusts came whistling out of the south, and meeting
these they were driven back westward again. The

clouds broke and boiled in the sky, and the ship's master roared out ragefully, "This fool's gale blows all ways at once! Only a magewind will get us through this weather, Lord."

Ged looked glum at that, but the ship and her men were in danger for him, so he raised up the magewind into her sail. At once the ship began to cleave straight to the east, and the ship's master began to look cheerful again. But little by little, though Ged kept up the spell, the magewind slackened, growing feebler, until the ship seemed to hang still on the waves for a minute, her sail drooping, amid all the tumult of the rain and gale. Then with a thundercrack the boom came swinging round and she jibed and jumped northward like a scared cat.

Ged grabbed hold of a stanchion, for she lay almost over on her side, and shouted out, "Turn back to Serd, master!"

The master cursed and shouted that he would not: "A wizard aboard, and I the best seaman of the Trade, and this the handiest ship I ever sailed—turn back?"

Then, the ship turning again almost as if a whirlpool had caught her keel, he too grabbed hold of the sternpost to keep aboard, and Ged said to him, "Leave me at Serd and sail where you like. It's not against your ship this wind blows, but against me."

"Against you, a wizard of Roke?"

"Have you never heard of the Roke-wind, master?"

"Aye, that keeps off evil powers from the Isle of the Wise, but what has that to do with you, a Dragontamer?"

"That is between me and my shadow," Ged answered shortly, as a wizard will; and he said no more as they went swiftly, with a steady wind and under clearing skies, back over the sea to Serd.

There was a heaviness and a dread in his heart as he went up from the wharves of Serd. The days were shortening into winter, and dusk came soon. With

dusk Ged's uneasiness always grew, and now the turning of each street seemed a threat to him, and he
had to steel himself not to keep looking back over his
shoulder at what might be coming behind him. He
went to the Sea-House of Serd, where travellers and
merchants ate together of good fare provided by the
township, and might sleep in the long raftered hall:
such is the hospitality of the thriving islands of the
Inmost Sea.

He saved a bit of meat from his dinner, and by the
firepit afterward he coaxed the otak out of the fold of
his hood where it had cowered all that day, and tried
to get it to eat, petting it and whispering to it, "Hoeg,
hoeg, little one, silent one. . . ." But it would not eat,
and crept into his pocket to hide. By that, by his own
dull uncertainty, by the very look of the darkness in
the corners of the great room, he knew that the
shadow was not far from him.

No one in this place knew him: they were travellers, from other isles, who had not heard the *Song of
the Sparrowhawk*. None spoke to him. He chose a
pallet at last and lay down, but all night long he lay
with open eyes there in the raftered hall among the
sleep of strangers. All night he tried to choose his
way, to plan where he should go, what he should do:
but each choice, each plan was blocked by a foreboding of doom. Across each way he might go lay the
shadow. Only Roke was clear of it: and to Roke he
could not go, forbidden by the high, enwoven, ancient spells that kept the perilous island safe. That
the Roke-wind had risen against him was proof the
thing that hunted him must be very close upon him
now.

That thing was bodiless, blind to sunlight, a creature of a lightless, placeless, timeless realm. It must
grope after him through the days and across the seas
of the sunlit world, and could take visible shape only
in dream and darkness. It had as yet no substance or
being that the light of the sun would shine on; and so

it is sung in the *Deed of Hode,* "Daybreak makes all
earth and sea, from shadow brings forth form, driving
dream to the dark kingdom." But if once the shadow
caught up with Ged it could draw his power out of
him, and take from him the very weight and warmth
and life of his body and the will that moved him.

That was the doom he saw lying ahead on every road. And he knew that he might be tricked
toward that doom; for the shadow, growing stronger
always as it was nearer him, might even now have
strength enough to put evil powers or evil men to its
own use—showing him false portents, or speaking
with a stranger's voice. For all he knew, in one of
these men who slept in this corner or that of the raftered hall of the Sea-House tonight, the dark thing
lurked, finding a foothold in a dark soul and there
waiting and watching Ged and feeding, even now, on
his weakness, on his uncertainty, on his fear.

It was past bearing. He must trust to chance, and
run wherever chance took him. At the first cold hint
of dawn he got up and went in haste under the dimming stars down to the wharves of Serd, resolved
only to take the first ship outward bound that would
have him. A galley was loading turbie-oil; she was to
sail at sunrise, bound for Havnor Great Port. Ged
asked passage of her master. A wizard's staff is pass-
port and payment on most ships. They took him
aboard willingly, and within that hour the ship set
forth. Ged's spirits lifted with the first lifting of the
forty long oars, and the drumbeat that kept the stroke
made a brave music to him.

And yet he did not know what he would do in
Havnor, or where he would run from there. Northward was as good as any direction. He was a
Northerner himself; maybe he would find some ship
to take him on to Gont from Havnor, and he might
see Ogion again. Or he might find some ship going
far out into the Reaches, so far the shadow would
lose him and give up the hunt. Beyond such vague

ideas as these, there was no plan in his head, and he saw no one course that he must follow. Only he must run. . . .

Those forty oars carried the ship over a hundred and fifty miles of wintry sea before sunset of the second day out from Serd. They came in to port at Orrimy on the east shore of the great land Hosk, for these trade-galleys of the Inmost Sea keep to the coasts and lie overnight in harbor whenever they can. Ged went ashore, for it was still daylight, and he roamed the steep streets of the port-town, aimless and brooding.

Orrimy is an old town, built heavily of stone and brick, walled against the lawless lords of the interior of Hosk Island; the warehouses on the docks are like forts, and the merchants' houses are towered and fortified. Yet to Ged wandering through the streets those ponderous mansions seemed like veils, behind which lay an empty dark; and people who passed him, intent on their business, seemed not real men but voiceless shadows of men. As the sun set he came down to the wharves again, and even there in the broad red light and wind of the day's end, sea and land alike to him seemed dim and silent.

"Where are you bound, Lord Wizard?"

So one hailed him suddenly from behind. Turning he saw a man dressed in grey, who carried a staff of heavy wood that was not a wizard's staff. The stranger's face was hidden by his hood from the red light, but Ged felt the unseen eyes meet his. Starting back he raised his own yew-staff between him and the stranger.

Mildly the man asked, "What do you fear?"

"What follows behind me."

"So? But I'm not your shadow."

Ged stood silent. He knew that indeed this man, whatever he was, was not what he feared: he was no shadow or ghost or gebbeth-creature. Amidst the dry silence and shadowiness that had come over the world, he even kept a voice and some solidity. He put back his hood now. He had a strange, seamed, bald head, a lined face. Though age had not sounded in his voice, he looked to be an old man.

"I do not know you," said the man in grey, "yet I think perhaps we do not meet by chance. I heard a tale once of a young man, a scarred man, who won through darkness to great dominion, even to kingship. I do not know if that is your tale. But I will tell you this: go to the Court of the Terrenon, if you need a sword to fight shadows with. A staff of yew-wood will not serve your need."

Hope and mistrust struggled in Ged's mind as he listened. A wizardly man soon learns that few indeed of his meetings are chance ones, be they for good or for ill.

"In what land is the Court of the Terrenon?"

"In Osskill."

At the sound of that name Ged saw for a moment, by a trick of memory, a black raven on green grass who looked up at him sidelong with an eye like polished stone, and spoke; but the words were forgotten.

"That land has something of a dark name," Ged said, looking ever at the man in grey, trying to judge what kind of man he was. There was a manner about him that hinted of the sorcerer, even of the wizard; and yet boldly as he spoke to Ged, there was a queer beaten look about him, the look almost of a sick man, or a prisoner, or a slave.

"You are from Roke," he answered. "The wizards of Roke give a dark name to wizardries other than their own."

"What man are you?"

"A traveller; a trader's agent from Osskil; I am here on business," said the man in grey. When Ged asked him no more he quietly bade the young man good night, and went off up the narrow stepped street above the quays.

Ged turned, irresolute whether to heed this sign or

not, and looked to the north. The red light was dying
out fast from the hills and from the windy sea. Grey
dusk came, and on its heels the night.

Ged went in sudden decision and haste along the
quays to a fisherman who was folding his nets down
in his dory, and hailed him: "Do you know any ship
in this port bound north—to Semel, or the Enlades?"

"The longship yonder's from Osskil, she might be
stopping at the Enlades."

In the same haste Ged went on to the great ship
the fisherman had pointed to, a longship of sixty oars,
gaunt as a snake, her high bent prow carven and inlaid with disks of loto-shell, her oarport-covers painted red, with the rune Sifl sketched on each in black.
A grim, swift ship she looked, and all in sea-trim,
with all her crew aboard. Ged sought out the ship's
master and asked passage to Osskil of him.

"Can you pay?"

"I have some skill with winds."

"I am a weatherworker myself. You have nothing to
give? no money?"

In Low Torning the Isle-Men had paid Ged as best
they could with the ivory pieces used by traders in
the Archipelago; he would take only ten pieces,
though they wanted to give him more. He offered
these now to the Osskilian, but he shook his head.
"We do not use those counters. If you have nothing to
pay, I have no place aboard for you."

"Do you need arms? I have rowed in a galley."

"Aye, we're short two men. Find your bench then,"
said the ship's master, and paid him no more heed.

So, laying his staff and his bag of books under the
rowers' bench, Ged became for ten bitter days of winter an oarsman of that Northern ship. They left Orrimy at daybreak, and that day Ged thought he could
never keep up his work. His left arm was somewhat
lamed by the old wounds in his shoulder, and all his
rowing in the channels about Low Torning had not
trained him for the relentless pull and pull and pull

at the long galley-oar to the beat of the drum. Each stint at the oars was of two or three hours, and then a second shift of oarsmen took the benches, but the time of rest seemed only long enough for all Ged's muscles to stiffen, and then it was back to the oars. And the second day of it was worse; but after that he hardened to the labor, and got on well enough.

There was no such comradeship among this crew as he had found aboard *Shadow* when he first went to Roke. The crewmen of Andradean and Gontish ships are partners in the trade, working together for a common profit, whereas traders of Osskil use slaves and bondsmen or hire men to row, paying them with small coins of gold. Gold is a great thing in Osskil. But it is not a source of good fellowship there, or amongst the dragons, who also prize it highly. Since half this crew were bondsmen, forced to work, the ship's officers were slavemasters, and harsh ones. They never laid their whips on the back of an oarsman who worked for pay or passage; but there will not be much friendliness in a crew of whom some are whipped and others are not. Ged's fellows said little to one another, and less to him. They were mostly men from Osskil, speaking not the Hardic tongue of the Archipelago but a dialect of their own, and they were dour men, pale-skinned with black drooping mustaches and lank hair. *Kelub*, the red one, was Ged's name among them. Though they knew he was a wizard they showed him no regard, but rather a kind of cautious spitefulness. And he himself was in no mood for making friends. Even on his bench, caught up in the mighty rhythm of the rowing, one oarsman among sixty in a ship racing over void grey seas, he felt himself exposed, defenseless. When they came into strange ports at nightfall and he rolled himself in his cloak to sleep, weary as he was he would dream, wake, dream again: evil dreams, that he could not recall waking, though they seemed to

hang about the ship and the men of the ship, so that
he mistrusted each one of them.

All the Osskilian freemen wore a long knife at the
hip, and one day as his oar-shift shared their noon
meal one of these men asked Ged, "Are you slave or
oathbreaker, Kelub?"

"Neither."

"Why no knife, then? Afraid to fight?" said the
man, Skiorh, jeering.

"No."

"Your little dog fight for you?"

"Otak," said another who listened. "No dog, that is
otak," and he said something in Osskilian that made
Skiorh scowl and turn away. Just as he turned Ged
saw a change in his face, a slurring and shifting of
the features, as if for a moment something had
changed him, used him, looking out through his eyes
sidelong at Ged. Yet the next minute Ged saw him
fullface, and he looked as usual, so that Ged told
himself that what he had seen was his own fear, his
own dread reflected in the other's eyes. But that night
as they lay in port in Esen he dreamed, and Skiorh
walked in his dream. Afterwards he avoided the man
as best he could, and it seemed also that Skiorh kept
away from him, and no more words passed between
them.

The snow-crowned mountains of Havnor sank away
behind them southward, blurred by the mists of early
winter. They rowed on past the mouth of the Sea of
Éa where long ago Elfarran was drowned, and past
the Enlades. They lay two days in port at Berila, the
City of Ivory, white above its bay in the west of
myth-haunted Enlad. At all ports they came to, the
crewmen were kept aboard the ship, and set no foot
on land. Then as a red sun rose they rowed out on
the Osskil Sea, into the northeast winds that blow
unhindered from the islandless vastness of the North
Reach. Through that bitter sea they brought their
cargo safe, coming the second day out of Berila into

port at Neshum, the trade-city of Eastern Osskil.

Ged saw a low coast lashed by rainy wind, a grey town crouching behind the long stone breakwaters that made its harbor, and behind the town treeless hills under a snow-darkened sky. They had come far from the sunlight of the Inmost Sea.

Longshoremen of the Sea-Guild of Neshum came aboard to unload the cargo—gold, silver, jewelry, fine silks and Southern tapestries, such precious stuff as the lords of Osskil hoard—and the freemen of the crew were dismissed. Ged stopped one of them to ask his way; up until now the distrust he felt of all of them had kept him from saying where he was bound, but now, afoot and alone in a strange land, he must ask for guidance. The man went on impatiently saying he did not know, but Skiorh, overhearing, said, "The Court of the Terrenon? On the Keksemt Moors. I go that road."

Skiorh's was no company Ged would have chosen, but knowing neither the language nor the way he had small choice. Nor did it much matter, he thought; he had not chosen to come here. He had been driven, and now was driven on. He pulled his hood up over his head, took up his staff and bag, and followed the Osskilian through the streets of the town and upward into the snowy hills. The little otak would not ride on his shoulder, but hid in the pocket of his sheepskin tunic, under his cloak, as was its wont in cold weather. The hills stretched out into bleak rolling moorlands as far as the eye could see. They walked in silence and the silence of winter lay on all the land.

"How far?" Ged asked after they had gone some miles, seeing no sight of village or farm in any direction, and thinking that they had no food with them. Skiorh turned his head a moment, pulling up his own hood, and said, "Not far."

It was an ugly face, pale, coarse, and cruel, but Ged feared no man, though he might fear where such a man would guide him. He nodded, and they went

on. Their road was only a scar through the waste of
thin snow and leafless bushes. From time to time
other tracks crossed it or branched from it. Now that
the chimney-smoke of Neshum was hidden behind
the hills in the darkening afternoon there was no sign
at all of what way they should go, or had gone. Only
the wind blew always from the east. And when they
had walked for several hours Ged thought he saw,
away off on the hills in the northwest where their
way tended, a tiny scratch against the sky, like a
tooth, white. But the light of the short day was fading, and on the next rise of the road he could make
out the thing, tower or tree or whatever, no more
clearly than before.

"Do we go there?" he asked, pointing.

Skiorh made no answer but plodded on, muffled in
his coarse cloak with its peaked, furred Osskilian
hood. Ged strode on beside him. They had come far,
and he was drowsy with the steady pace of their
walking and with the long weariness of hard days
and nights in the ship. It began to seem to him that
he had walked forever and would walk forever beside
this silent being through a silent darkening land. Cau-
tion and intention were dulled in him. He walked as
in a long, long dream, going no place.

The otak stirred in his pocket, and a little vague
fear also woke and stirred in his mind. He forced himself to speak. "Darkness comes, and snow. How far,
Skiorh?"

After a pause the other answered, without turning,
"Not far."

But his voice sounded not like a man's voice, but
like a beast, hoarse and lipless, that tries to speak.

Ged stopped. All around stretched empty hills in
the late, dusk light. Sparse snow whirled a little falling. "Skiorh!" he said, and the other halted, and
turned. There was no face under the peaked hood.

. Before Ged could speak spell or summon power,
the gebbeth spoke, saying in its hoarse voice, "Ged!"

Then the young man could work no transformation, but was locked in his true being, and must face the gebbeth thus defenseless. Nor could he summon any help in this alien land, where nothing and no one was known to him and would come at his call. He stood alone, with nothing between him and his enemy but the staff of yew-wood in his right hand.

The thing that had devoured Skiorh's mind and possessed his flesh made the body take a step towards Ged, and the arms came groping out towards him. A rage of horror filled Ged and he swung up and brought down his staff whistling on the hood that hid the shadow-face. Hood and cloak collapsed down nearly to the ground under that fierce blow as if there was nothing in them but wind, and then writhing and flapping stood up again. The body of a gebbeth has been drained of true substance and is something like a shell or a vapor in the form of a man, an unreal flesh clothing the shadow which is real. So jerking and billowing as if blown on the wind the shadow spread its arms and came at Ged, trying to get hold of him as it had held him on Roke Knoll: and if it did it would cast aside the husk of Skiorh and enter into Ged, devouring him out from within, owning him, which was its whole desire. Ged struck at it again with his heavy, smoking staff, beating it off, but it came again and he struck again, and then dropped the staff that blazed and smouldered, burning his hand. He backed away, then all at once turned and ran.

He ran, and the gebbeth followed a pace behind him, unable to outrun him yet never dropping behind. Ged never looked back. He ran, he ran, through that vast dusk land where there was no hiding place. Once the gebbeth in its hoarse whistling voice called him again by name, but though it had taken his wizard's power thus, it had no power over his body's strength, and could not make him stop. He ran.

Night thickened about the hunter and the hunted,

and snow blew fine across the path that Ged could no
longer see. The pulse hammered in his eyes, the
breath burned in his throat, he was no longer really
running but stumbling and staggering ahead: and yet
the tireless pursuer seemed unable to catch up, coming always just behind him. It had begun to whisper
and mumble at him, calling to him, and he knew that
all his life that whispering had been in his ears, just
under the threshold of hearing, but now he could
hear it, and he must yield, he must give in, he must
stop. Yet he labored on, struggling up a long, dim
slope. He thought there was a light somewhere before
him, and he thought he heard a voice in front of him,
above him somewhere, calling, "Come! Come!"

   He tried to answer but he had no voice. The pale
light grew certain, shining through a gateway straight
before him: he could not see the walls, but he saw
the gate. At the sight of it he halted, and the gebbeth
snatched at his cloak, fumbled at his sides trying to
catch hold of him from behind. With the last strength
in him Ged plunged through that faint-shining door.
He tried to turn to shut it behind him against the
gebbeth, but his legs would not hold him up. He
staggered, reaching for support. Lights swam and
flashed in his eyes. He felt himself falling, and he felt
himself caught even as he fell; but his mind, utterly
spent, slid away into the dark.

# 7 The Hawk's Flight

Ged woke, and for a long time he lay aware only that it was pleasant to wake, for he had not expected to wake again, and very pleasant to see light, the large plain light of day all about him. He felt as if he were floating on that light, or drifting in a boat on very quiet waters. At last he made out that he was in bed, but no such bed as he had ever slept in. It was set up on a frame held by four tall carven legs, and the mattresses were great silk sacks of down, which was why he thought he was floating, and over it all a crimson canopy hung to keep out drafts. On two sides the curtain was tied back, and Ged looked out at a room with walls of stone and floor of stone. Through three high windows he saw the moorland, bare and brown, snow-patched here and there, in the mild sunlight of winter. The room must be high above the ground, for it looked a great way over the land.

A coverlet of downfilled satin slid aside as Ged sat up, and he saw himself clothed in a tunic of silk and cloth-of-silver like a lord. On a chair beside the bed, boots of glove-leather and a cloak lined with pellawi-fur were laid ready for him. He sat a while, calm and dull as one under an enchantment, and then stood up, reaching for his staff. But he had no staff.

His right hand, though it had been salved and bound, was burned on palm and fingers. Now he felt the pain of it, and the soreness of all his body.

He stood without moving a while again. Then he whispered, not aloud and not hopefully, "Hoeg ... hoeg ..." For the little fierce loyal creature too was gone, the little silent soul that once had led him back from death's dominion. Had it still been with him last night when he ran? Was that last night, was it many nights ago? He did not know. It was all dim and obscure in his mind, the gebbeth, the burning staff, the running, the whispering, the gate. None of it came back clearly to him. Nothing even now was clear. He whispered his pet's name once more, but without hope of answer, and tears rose in his eyes.

A little bell rang somewhere far away. A second bell rang in a sweet jangle just outside the room. A door opened behind him, across the room, and a woman came in. "Welcome, Sparrowhawk," she said smiling.

She was young and tall, dressed in white and silver, with a net of silver crowning her hair that fell straight down like a fall of black water.

Stiffly Ged bowed.

"You don't remember me, I think."

"Remember you, Lady?"

He had never seen a beautiful woman dressed to match her beauty but once in his life: that Lady of O who had come with her Lord to the Sunreturn festival at Roke. She had been like a slight, bright candle-flame, but this woman was like the white new moon.

"I thought you would not," she said smiling. "But forgetful as you may be, you're welcome here as an old friend."

"What place is this?" Ged asked, still stiff and slow-tongued. He found it hard to speak to her and hard to look away from her. The princely clothes he wore were strange to him, the stones he stood on were unfamiliar, the very air he breathed was alien; he was not himself, not the self he had been.

"This keep is called the Court of the Terrenon. My lord, who is called Benderesk, is sovereign of this land from the edge of the Keksemt Moors north to the Mountains of Os, and keeper of the precious stone called Terrenon. As for myself, here in Osskil they call me Serret, Silver in their language. And you, I know, are sometimes called Sparrowhawk, and were made wizard in the Isle of the Wise."

Ged looked down at his burned hand and said presently, "I do not know what I am. I had power, once. I have lost it, I think."

"No! you have not lost it, or only to regain it ten-fold. You are safe here from what drove you here, my friend. There are mighty walls about this tower and not all of them are built of stone. Here you can rest, finding your strength again. Here you may also find a different strength, and a staff that will not burn to ashes in your hand. An evil way may lead to a good end, after all. Come with me now, let me show you our domain."

She spoke so sweetly that Ged hardly heard her words, moved by the promise of her voice alone. He followed her.

His room was high up indeed in the tower that rose like a sharp tooth from its hilltop. Down winding stairs of marble he followed Serret, through rich rooms and halls, past high windows that looked north, west, south, east over the low brown hills that went on, houseless and treeless and changeless, clear to the sunwashed winter sky. Only far to the north small white peaks stood sharp against the blue, and southward one could guess the shining of the sea.

Servants opened doors and stood aside for Ged and

the lady; pale, dour Osskilians they were all. She was
light of skin, but unlike them she spoke Hardic well,
even, it seemed to Ged, with the accent of Gont. Later
that day she brought him before her husband Benderesk, Lord of the Terrenon. Thrice her age, bone-
white, bone-thin, with clouded eyes, Lord Benderesk
greeted Ged with grim cold courtesy, bidding him
stay as guest however long he would. Then he had
little more to say, asking Ged nothing of his voyages
or of the enemy that had hunted him here; nor had
the Lady Serret asked anything of these matters.

If this was strange, it was only part of the strangeness of this place and of his presence in it. Ged's
mind never seemed quite to clear. He could not see
things plainly. He had come to this tower-keep by
chance, and yet the chance was all design; or he had
come by design and yet all the design had merely
chanced to come about. He had set out northward; a
stranger in Orrimy had told him to seek help here; an
Osskilian ship had been waiting for him; Skiorh had
guided him. How much of this was the work of the
shadow that hunted him? Or was none of it; had he
and his hunter both been drawn here by some other
power, he following that lure and the shadow following him, and seizing on Skiorh for its weapon when
the moment came? That must be it, for certainly the
shadow was, as Serret had said, barred from the
Court of the Terrenon. He had felt no sign or threat
of its lurking presence since he wakened in the tower.
But what then had brought him here? For this was no
place one came to by chance; even in the dullness of
his thoughts he began to see that. No other stranger
came to these gates. The tower stood aloof and remote, its back turned on the way to Neshum that was
the nearest town. No man came to the keep, none left
it. Its windows looked down on desolation.

From these windows Ged looked out, as he kept by
himself in his high tower-room, day after day, dull
and heartsick and cold. It was always cold in the

tower, for all the carpets and the tapestried hangings and the rich furred clothing and the broad marble fireplaces they had. It was a cold that got into the bone, into the marrow, and would not be dislodged. And in Ged's heart a cold shame settled also and would not be dislodged, as he thought always how he had faced his enemy and been defeated and had run. In his mind all the Masters of Roke gathered, Gensher the Archmage frowning in their midst, and Nemmerle was with them, and Ogion, and even the witch who had taught him his first spell: all of them gazed at him and he knew he had failed their trust in him. He would plead, saying, "If I had not run away the shadow would have possessed me: it had already all Skiorh's strength, and part of mine, and I could not fight it: it knew my name. I had to run away. A wizard-gebbeth would be a terrible power for evil and ruin. I had to run away." But none of those who listened in his mind would answer him. And he would watch the snow falling, thin and ceaseless, on the empty lands below the window, and feel the dull cold grow within him, till it seemed no feeling was left to him except a kind of weariness.

So he kept to himself for many days out of sheer misery. When he did come down out of his room, he was silent and stiff. The beauty of the Lady of the Keep confused his mind, and in this rich, seemly, orderly, strange Court, he felt himself to be a goatherd born and bred.

They let him alone when he wanted to be alone, and when he could not stand to think his thoughts and watch the falling snow any longer, often Serret met with him in one of the curving halls, tapestried and firelit, lower in the tower, and there they would talk. There was no merriment in the Lady of the Keep, she never laughed though she often smiled; yet she could put Ged at ease almost with one smile. With her he began to forget his stiffness and his shame. Before long they met every day to talk, long, quietly, idly, a little apart from the serving-women who always accompanied Serret, by the fireplace or at the window of the high rooms of the tower.

The old lord kept mostly in his own apartments, coming forth mornings to pace up and down the snowy inner courtyards of the castle-keep like an old sorcerer who has been brewing spells all night. When he joined Ged and Serret for supper he sat silent, looking up at his young wife sometimes with a hard, covetous glance. Then Ged pitied her. She was like a white deer caged, like a white bird wing-clipped, like a silver ring on an old man's finger. She was an item of Benderesk's hoard. When the lord of the keep left them Ged stayed with her, trying to cheer her solitude as she had cheered his.

"What is this jewel that gives your keep its name?" he asked her as they sat talking over their emptied gold plates and gold goblets in the carvernous, candle-lit dining-hall.

"You have not heard of it? It is a famous thing."

"No. I know only that the lords of Osskil have famous treasuries."

"Ah, this jewel outshines them all. Come, would you like to see it?"

She smiled, with a look of mockery and daring, as if a little afraid of what she did, and led the young man from the hall, out through the narrow corridors of the base of the tower, and down stairs underground to a locked door he had not seen before. This she unlocked with a silver key, looking up at Ged with that same smile as she did so, as if she dared him to come on with her. Beyond the door was a short passage and a second door, which she unlocked with a gold key, and beyond that again a third door, which she unlocked with one of the Great Words of unbinding. Within that last door her candle showed them a small room like a dungeon-cell: floor, walls, ceiling all rough stone, unfurnished, blank.

"Do you see it?" Serret asked.

As Ged looked round the room his wizard's eye caught one stone of those that made the floor. It was rough and dank as the rest, a heavy unshapen paving-stone: yet he felt the power of it as if it spoke to him aloud. And his breath caught in his throat, and a sickness came over him for a moment. This was the foundingstone of the tower. This was the central place, and it was cold, bitter cold; nothing could ever warm the little room. This was a very ancient thing: an old and terrible spirit was prisoned in that block of stone. He did not answer Serret yes or no, but stood still, and presently, with a quick curious glance at him, she pointed out the stone. "That is the Terrenon. Do you wonder that we keep so precious a jewel locked away in our deepest hoardroom?"

Still Ged did not answer, but stood dumb and wary. She might almost have been testing him; but he thought she had no notion of the stone's nature, to speak of it so lightly. She did not know enough of it to fear it. "Tell me of its powers," he said at last.

"It was made before Segoy raised the islands of the world from the Open Sea. It was made when the world itself was made, and will endure until the end of the world. Time is nothing to it. If you lay your hand upon it and ask a question of it, it will answer, according to the power that is in you. It has a voice, if you know how to listen. It will speak of things that were, and are, and will be. It told of your coming, long before you came to this land. Will you ask a question of it now?"

"No."

"It will answer you."

"There is no question I would ask it."

"It might tell you," Serret said in her soft voice, "how you will defeat your enemy."

Ged stood mute.

"Do you fear the stone?" she asked as if unbelieving; and he answered, "Yes."

In the deadly cold and silence of the room encircled by wall after wall of spellwork and of stone, in the light of the one candle she held, Serret glanced at him again with gleaming eyes. "Sparrowhawk," she said, "you are not afraid."

"But I will not speak with that spirit," Ged replied, and looking full at her spoke with a grave boldness: "My lady, that spirit is sealed in a stone, and the stone is locked by binding-spell and blinding-spell and charm of lock and ward and triple fortress-walls in a barren land, not because it is precious, but because it can work great evil. I do not know what they told you of it when you came here. But you who are young and gentle-hearted should never touch the thing, or even look on it. It will not work you well."

"I have touched it. I have spoken to it, and heard it speak. It does me no harm."

She turned away and they went out through the doors and passages till in the torchlight of the broad stairs of the tower she blew out her candle. They parted with few words.

That night Ged slept little. It was not the thought of the shadow that kept him awake; rather that thought was almost driven from his mind by the image, ever returning, of the Stone on which this tower was founded, and by the vision of Serret's face bright and shadowy in the candle-light, turned to him. Again and again he felt her eyes on him, and tried to decide what look had come into those eyes when he refused to touch the Stone, whether it had been disdain or hurt. When he lay down to sleep at last the silken sheets of the bed were cold as ice, and ever he wakened in the dark thinking of the Stone and of Serret's eyes.

Next day he found her in the curving hall of grey marble, lit now by the westering sun, where often she spent the afternoon at games or at the weaving-loom with her maids. He said to her, "Lady Serret, I affronted you. I am sorry for it."

"No," she said musingly, and again, "No...." She

sent away the serving-women who were with her, and when they were alone she turned to Ged. "My guest, my friend," she said, "you are very clear-sighted, but perhaps you do not see all that is to be seen. In Gont, in Roke they teach high wizardries. But they do not teach all wizardries. This is Osskil, Ravenland: it is not a Hardic land: mages do not rule it, nor do they know much of it. There are happenings here not dealt with by the loremasters of the South, and things here not named in the Namers' lists. What one does not know, one fears. But you have nothing to fear here in the Court of the Terrenon. A weaker man would, indeed. Not you. You are one born with the power to control that which is in the sealed room. This I know. It is why you are here now."

"I do not understand."

"That is because my lord Benderesk has not been wholly frank with you. I will be frank. Come, sit by me here."

He sat down beside her on the deep, cushioned window-ledge. The dying sunlight came level through the window, flooding them with a radiance in which there was no warmth; on the moorlands below, already sinking into shadow, last night's snow lay unmelted, a dull white pall over the earth.

She spoke now very softly. "Benderesk is Lord and Inheritor of the Terrenon, but he cannot use the thing, he cannot make it wholly serve his will. Nor can I, alone or with him. Neither he nor I has the skill and power. You have both."

"How do you know that?"

"From the Stone itself! I told you that it spoke of your coming. It knows its master. It has waited for you to come. Before ever you were born it waited for you, for the one who could master it. And he who can make the Terrenon answer what he asks and do what he wills, has power over his own destiny: strength to crush any enemy, mortal or of the other world: foresight, knowledge, wealth, dominion, and a wizardry

at his command that could humble the Archmage
himself! As much of that, as little of that as you
choose, is yours for the asking."

Once more she lifted her strange bright eyes to
him, and her gaze pierced him so that he trembled as
if with cold. Yet there was fear in her face, as if she
sought his help but was too proud to ask it. Ged was
bewildered. She had put her hand on his as she
spoke; its touch was light, it looked narrow and fair
on his dark, strong hand. He said, pleading, "Serret! I
have no such power as you think—what I had once, I
threw away. I cannot help you, I am no use to you.
But I know this, the Old Powers of earth are not for
men to use. They were never given into our hands,
and in our hands they work only ruin. Ill means, ill
end. I was not drawn here, but driven here, and the
force that drove me works to my undoing. I cannot
help you."

"He who throws away his power is filled sometimes
with a far greater power," she said, smiling, as if his
fears and scruples were childish ones. "I may know
more than you of what brought you here. Did not a
man speak to you in the streets of Orrimy? He was a
messenger, a servant of the Terrenon. He was a
wizard once himself, but he threw away his staff to
serve a power greater than any mage's. And you
came to Osskil, and on the moors you tried to fight a
shadow with your wooden staff; and almost we could
not save you, for that thing that follows you is more
cunning than we deemed, and had taken much
strength from you already.... Only shadow can fight
shadow. Only darkness can defeat the dark. Listen,
Sparrowhawk! what do you need, then, to defeat that
shadow, which waits for you outside these walls?"

"I need what I cannot know. Its name."

"The Terrenon, that knows all births and deaths
and beings before and after death, the unborn and
the undying, the bright world and the dark one, will
tell you that name."

"And the price?"

"There is no price. I tell you it will obey you, serve you as your slave."

Shaken and tormented, he did not answer. She held his hand now in both of hers, looking into his face. The sun had fallen into the mists that dulled the horizon, and the air too had grown dull, but her face grew bright with praise and triumph as she watched him and saw his will shaken within him. Softly she whispered, "You will be mightier than all men, a king among men. You will rule, and I will rule with you—"

Suddenly Ged stood up, and one step forward took him where he could see, just around the curve of the long room's wall, beside the door, the Lord of the Terrenon who stood listening and smiling a little.

Ged's eyes cleared, and his mind. He looked down at Serret. "It is light that defeats the dark," he said stammering,—"light."

As he spoke he saw, as plainly as if his own words were the light that showed him, how indeed he had been drawn here, lured here, how they had used his fear to lead him on, and how they would, once they had him, have kept him. They had saved him from the shadow, indeed, for they did not want him to be possessed by the shadow until he had become a slave of the Stone. Once his will was captured by the power of the Stone, then they would let the shadow into the walls, for a gebbeth was a better slave even than a man. If he had once touched the Stone, or spoken to it, he would have been utterly lost. Yet, even as the shadow had not quite been able to catch up with him and seize him, so the Stone had not been able to use him—not quite. He had almost yielded, but not quite. He had not consented. It is very hard for evil to take hold of the unconsenting soul.

He stood between the two who had yielded, who had consented, looking from one to the other as Benderesk came forward.

"I told you," the Lord of the Terrenon said dryvoiced to his lady, "that he would slip from your hands, Serret. They are clever fools, your Gontish sorcerers. And you are a fool too, woman of Gont, thinking to trick both him and me, and rule us both by your beauty, and use the Terrenon to your own ends. But I am the Lord of the Stone, I, and this I do to the disloyal wife: *Ekavroe ai oelwantar—*" It was a spell of Changing, and Benderesk's long hands were raised to shape the cowering woman into some hideous thing, swine or dog or drivelling hag. Ged stepped forward and struck the lord's hands down with his own, saying as he did so only one short word. And though he had no staff, and stood on alien ground and evil ground, the domain of a dark power, yet his will prevailed. Benderesk stood still, his clouded eyes fixed hateful and unseeing upon Serret.

"Come," she said in a shaking voice, "Sparrowhawk, come, quick, before he can summon the Servants of the Stone—"

As if in echo a whispering ran through the tower, through the stones of the floor and walls, a dry trembling murmur, as if the earth itself should speak.

Seizing Ged's hand Serret ran with him through the passages and halls, down the long twisted stairs. They came out into the courtyard where a last silvery daylight still hung above the soiled, trodden snow. Three of the castle-servants barred their way, sullen and questioning, as if they had been suspecting some plot of these two against their master. "It grows dark, Lady," one said, and another, "You cannot ride out now."

"Out of my way, filth!" Serret cried, and spoke in the sibilant Osskilian speech. The men fell back from her and crouched down to the ground, writhing, and one of them screamed aloud.

"We must go out by the gate, there is no other way out. Can you see it? can you find it, Sparrowhawk?"

She tugged at his hand, yet he hesitated. "What spell did you set on them?"

"I ran hot lead in the marrow of their bones, they will die of it. Quick, I tell you, he will loose the Servants of the Stone, and I cannot find the gate—there is a great charm on it. Quick!"

Ged did not know what she meant, for to him the enchanted gate was as plain to see as the stone archway of the court through which he saw it. He led Serret through the one, across the untrodden snow of the forecourt, and then, speaking a word of Opening, he led her through the gate of the wall of spells.

She changed as they passed through that doorway out of the silvery twilight of the Court of the Terrenon. She was not less beautiful in the drear light of the moors, but there was a fierce witch-look to her beauty; and Ged knew her at last—the daughter of the Lord of the Re Albi, daughter of a sorceress of Osskil, who had mocked him in the green meadows above Ogion's house, long ago, and had sent him to read that spell which loosed the shadow. But he spent small thought on this, for he was looking about him now with every sense alert, looking for that enemy, the shadow, which would be waiting for him somewhere outside the magic walls. It might be gebbeth still, clothed in Skiorh's death, or it might be hidden in the gathering darkness, waiting to seize him and merge its shapelessness with his living flesh. He sensed its nearness, yet did not see it. But as he looked he saw some small dark thing half buried in snow, a few paces from the gate. He stooped, and then softly picked it up in his two hands. It was the otak, its fine short fur all clogged with blood and its small body light and stiff and cold in his hands.

"Change yourself! Change yourself, they are coming!" Serret shrieked, seizing his arm and pointing to the tower that stood behind them like a tall white tooth in the dusk. From slit windows near its base dark creatures were creeping forth, flapping long wings, slowly beating and circling up over the walls towards Ged and Serret where they stood on the hillside, unprotected. The rattling whisper they had heard inside the keep had grown louder, a tremor and moaning in the earth under their feet.

Anger welled up in Ged's heart, a hot rage of hate against all the cruel deathly things that tricked him, trapped him, hunted him down. "Change yourself!" Serret screamed at him, and she with a quick-gasped spell shrank into a grey gull, and flew. But Ged stooped and plucked a blade of wild grass that poked up dry and frail out of the snow where the otak had lain dead. This blade he held up, and as he spoke aloud to it in the True Speech it lengthened, and thickened, and when he was done he held a great staff, a wizard's staff, in his hand. No banefire burned red along it when the black, flapping creatures from the Court of the Terrenon swooped over him and he struck their wings with it: it blazed only with the white magefire that does not burn but drives away the dark.

The creatures returned to the attack: botched beasts, belonging to ages before bird or dragon or man, long since forgotten by the daylight but recalled by the ancient, malign, unforgetful power of the Stone. They harried Ged, swooping at him. He felt the scythe-sweep of their talons about him and sickened in their dead stench. Fiercely he parried and struck, fighting them off with the fiery staff that was made of his anger and a blade of wild grass. And suddenly they all rose up like ravens frightened from carrion and wheeled away, flapping, silent, in the direction that Serret in her gull-shape had flown. Their vast wings seemed slow, but they flew fast, each downbeat driving them mightily through the air. No gull could long outmatch that heavy speed.

Quick as he had once done at Roke, Ged took the shape of a great hawk: not the sparrowhawk they called him but the Pilgrim Falcon that flies like arrow, like thought. On barred, sharp, strong wings he flew, pursuing his pursuers. The air darkened and among the clouds stars shone brightening. Ahead he saw the black ragged flock all driving down and in upon one point in mid-air. Beyond that black clot the sea lay, pale with last ashy gleam of day. Swift and straight the hawk-Ged shot towards the creatures of the Stone, and they scattered as he came amongst them as waterdrops scatter from a cast pebble. But they had caught their prey. Blood was on the beak of this one and white feathers stuck to the claws of another, and no gull skimmed beyond them over the pallid sea.

Already they were turning on Ged again, coming quick and ungainly with iron beaks stretched out agape. He, wheeling once above them, screamed the hawk's scream of defiant rage, and then shot on across the low beaches of Osskil, out over the breakers of the sea.

The creatures of the Stone circled a while croaking, and one by one beat back ponderously inland over the moors. The Old Powers will not cross over the sea, being bound each to an isle, a certain place, cave or stone or welling spring. Back went the black emanations to the tower-keep, where maybe the Lord of the Terrenon, Benderesk, wept at their return, and maybe laughed. But Ged went on, falcon-winged, falcon-mad, like an unfalling arrow, like an unforgotten thought, over the Osskil Sea and eastward into the wind of winter and the night.

Ogion the Silent had come home late to Re Albi from his autumn wanderings. More silent, more solitary than ever he had become as the years went on. The new Lord of Gont down in the city below had never got a word out of him, though he had climbed clear up to the Falcon's Nest to seek the help of the mage in a certain piratic venture towards the Andrades. Ogion who spoke to spiders on their webs and had been seen to greet trees courteously never said a word to the Lord of the Isle, who went away discontented. There was perhaps some discontent or unease also in Ogion's mind, for he had spent all summer and autumn alone up on the mountain, and only now near Sunreturn was come back to his hearthside.

The morning after his return he rose late, and wanting a cup of rushwash tea he went out to fetch water from the spring that ran a little way down the hillside from his house. The margins of the spring's small lively pool were frozen, and the sere moss among the rocks was traced with flowers of frost. It was broad daylight, but the sun would not clear the mighty shoulder of the mountain for an hour yet: all western Gont, from sea-beaches to the peak, was sunless, silent, and clear in the winter morning. As the mage stood by the spring looking out over the falling lands and the harbor and the grey distances of the sea, wings beat above him. He looked up, raising one arm a little. A great hawk came down with loud-beating wings and lighted on his wrist. Like a trained hunting-bird it clung there, but it wore no broken leash, no band or bell. The claws dug hard in Ogion's wrist; the barred wings trembled; the round, gold eye was dull and wild.

"Are you messenger or message?" Ogion said gently to the hawk. "Come on with me—" As he spoke the hawk looked at him. Ogion was silent a minute. "I named you once, I think," he said, and then strode to his house and entered, bearing the bird still on his wrist. He made the hawk stand on the hearth in the fire's heat, and offered it water. It would not drink. Then Ogion began to lay a spell, very quietly, weaving the web of magic with his hands more than with words. When the spell was whole and woven he said softly,—"Ged,"—not looking at the falcon on the hearth. He waited some while, then turned, and got up, and went to the young man who stood trembling and dull-eyed before the fire.

Ged was richly and outlandishly dressed in fur and

silk and silver, but the clothes were torn and stiff with sea-salt, and he stood gaunt and stooped, his hair lank about his scarred face.

Ogion took the soiled, princely cloak off his shoulders, led him to the alcove-room where his prentice once had slept and made him lie down on the pallet there, and so with a murmured sleep-charm left him. He had said no word to him, knowing that Ged had no human speech in him now.

As a boy, Ogion like all boys had thought it would be a very pleasant game to take by art-magic whatever shape one liked, man or beast, tree or cloud, and so to play at a thousand beings. But as a wizard he had learned the price of the game, which is the peril of losing one's self, playing away the truth. The longer a man stays in a form not his own, the greater this peril. Every prentice-sorcerer learns the tale of the wizard Bordger of Way, who delighted in taking bear's shape, and did so more and more often until the bear grew in him and the man died away, and he became a bear, and killed his own little son in the forests, and was hunted down and slain. And no one knows how many of the dolphins that leap in the waters of the Inmost Sea were men once, wise men, who forgot their wisdom and their name in the joy of the restless sea.

Ged had taken hawk-shape in fierce distress and rage, and when he flew from Osskil there had been but one thought in his mind: to outfly both Stone and shadow, to escape the cold treacherous lands, to go home. The falcon's anger and wildness were like his own, and had become his own, and his will to fly had become the falcon's will. Thus he had passed over Enlad, stooping down to drink at a lonely forest pool, but on the wing again at once, driven by fear of the shadow that came behind him. So he had crossed the great sea-lane called the Jaws of Enlad, and gone on and on, east by south, the hills of Oranéa faint to his

right and the hills of Andrad fainter to his left, and
before him only the sea; until at last, ahead, there
rose up out of the waves one unchanging wave, tow-
ering always higher, the white peak of Gont. In all
the sunlight and the dark of that great flight he had
worn the falcon's wings, and looked through the falcon's eyes, and forgetting his own thoughts he had
known at last only what the falcon knows: hunger,
the wind, the way he flies.

He flew to the right haven. There were few on
Roke and only one on Gont who could have made
him back into a man.

He was savage and silent when he woke. Ogion
never spoke to him, but gave him meat and water
and let him sit hunched by the fire, grim as a great,
weary, sulking hawk. When night came he slept. On
the third morning he came in to the fireside where
the mage sat gazing at the flames, and said,
"Master. . . ."

"Welcome, lad," said Ogion.

"I have come back to you as I left: a fool," the
young man said, his voice harsh and thickened. The
mage smiled a little and motioned Ged to sit across
the hearth from him, and set to brewing them some
tea.

Snow was falling, the first of the winter here on the
lower slopes of Gont. Ogion's windows were shut-
tered fast, but they could hear the wet snow as it fell
soft on the roof, and the deep stillness of snow all
about the house. A long time they sat there by the
fire, and Ged told his old master the tale of the years
since he had sailed from Gont aboard the ship called
*Shadow*. Ogion asked no questions, and when Ged
was done he kept silent for a long time, calm, pondering. Then he rose, and set out bread and cheese and
wine on the table, and they ate together. When they
had done and had set the room straight, Ogion spoke.

"Those are bitter scars you bear, lad," he said.

"I have no strength against the thing," Ged answered.

Ogion shook his head but said no more for a time. At length, "Strange," he said: "You had strength enough to outspell a sorcerer in his own domain, there in Osskil. You had strength enough to withstand the lures and fend off the attack of the servants of an Old Power of Earth. And at Pendor you had strength enough to stand up to a dragon."

"It was luck I had in Osskil, not strength," Ged replied, and he shivered again as he thought of the dreamlike deathly cold of the Court of the Terrenon. "As for the dragon, I knew his name. The evil thing, the shadow that hunts me, has no name."

"*All* things have a name," said Ogion, so certainly that Ged dared not repeat what the Archmage Gensher had told him, that such evil forces as he had loosed were nameless. The Dragon of Pendor, indeed, had offered to tell him the shadow's name, but he put little trust in the truth of that offer, nor did he believe Serret's promise that the Stone would tell him what he needed to know.

"If the shadow has a name," he said at last, "I do not think it will stop and tell it to me. . . ."

"No," said Ogion. "Nor have you stopped and told it your name. And yet it knew it. On the moors in Osskil it called you by your name, the name I gave you. It is strange, strange. . . ."

He fell to brooding again. At last Ged said, "I came here for counsel, not for refuge, Master. I will not bring this shadow upon you, and it will soon be here if I stay. Once you drove it from this very room—"

"No; that was but the foreboding of it, the shadow of a shadow. I could not drive it forth, now. Only you could do that."

"But I am powerless before it. Is there any place . . ." His voice died away before he had asked the question.

"There is no safe place," Ogion said gently. "Do not transform yourself again, Ged. The shadow seeks to destroy your true being. It nearly did so, driving you into hawk's being. No, where you should go, I do not know. Yet I have an idea of what you should do. It is a hard thing to say to you."

Ged's silence demanded truth, and Ogion said at last, "You must turn around."

"Turn around?"

"If you go ahead, if you keep running, wherever you run you will meet danger and evil, for it drives you, it chooses the way you go. You must choose. You must seek what seeks you. You must hunt the hunter."

Ged said nothing.

"At the spring of the River Ar I named you," the mage said, "a stream that falls from the mountain to the sea. A man would know the end he goes to, but he cannot know it if he does not turn, and return to his beginning, and hold that beginning in his being. If he would not be a stick whirled and whelmed in the stream, he must be the stream itself, all of it, from its spring to its sinking in the sea. You returned to Gont, you returned to me, Ged. Now turn clear round, and seek the very source, and that which lies before the source. There lies your hope of strength."

"There, Master?" Ged said with terror in his voice—"Where?"

Ogion did not answer.

"If I turn," Ged said after some time had gone by, "if as you say I hunt the hunter, I think the hunt will not be long. All its desire is to meet me face to face. And twice it has done so, and twice defeated me."

"Third time is the charm," said Ogion.

Ged paced the room up and down, from fireside to door, from door to fireside. "And if it defeats me wholly," he said, arguing perhaps with Ogion perhaps with himself, "it will take my knowledge and my power, and use them. It threatens only me, now. But if it enters into me and possesses me, it will work great evil through me."

"That is true. If it defeats you."

"Yet if I run again, it will as surely find me again. . . . And all my strength is spent in the running." Ged paced on a while, and then suddenly turned, and kneeling down before the mage he said, "I have walked with great wizards and have lived on the Isle of the Wise, but you are my true master, Ogion." He spoke with love, and with a somber joy.

"Good," said Ogion. "Now you know it. Better now than never. But you will be my master, in the end." He got up, and built up the fire to a good blaze, and hung the kettle over it to boil, and then pulling on his sheepskin coat said, "I must go look after my goats. Watch the kettle for me, lad."

When he came back in, all snow-powdered and stamping snow from his goatskin boots, he carried a long, rough shaft of yew-wood. All the end of the short afternoon, and again after their supper, he sat working by lampfire on the shaft with knife and rubbing-stone and spell-craft. Many times he passed his hands along the wood as if seeking any flaw. Often as he worked he sang softly. Ged, still weary, listened, and as he grew sleepy he thought himself a child in the witch's hut in Ten Alders village, on a snowy night in the firelit dark, the air heavy with herb-scent and smoke, and his mind all adrift on dreams as he listened to the long soft singing of spells and deeds of heroes who fought against dark powers and won, or lost, on distant islands long ago.

"There," said Ogion, and handed the finished staff to him. "The Archmage gave you yew-wood, a good choice and I kept to it. I meant the shaft for a longbow, but it's better this way. Good night, my son."

As Ged, who found no words to thank him, turned away to his alcove-room, Ogion watched him and said, too soft for Ged to hear, "O my young falcon, fly well!"

In the cold dawn when Ogion woke, Ged was gone. Only he had left in wizardly fashion a message of silver-scrawled runes on the hearthstone, that faded even as Ogion read them: "Master, I go hunting."

# 8 Hunting

Ged had set off down the road from Re Albi in the winter dark before sunrise, and before noon he came to the Port of Gont. Ogion had given him decent Gontish leggings and shirt and vest of leather and linen to replace his Osskilian finery, but Ged had kept for his winter journey the lordly cloak lined with pellawi-fur. So cloaked, empty-handed but for the dark staff that matched his height, he came to the Land Gate, and the soldiers lounging against the carven dragons there did not have to look twice at him to see the wizard. They drew aside their lances and let him enter without question, and watched him as he went on down the street.

On the quays and in the House of the Sea-Guild he asked of ships that might be going out north or west to Enlad, Andrad, Oranéa. All answered him that no ship would be leaving Gont Port now, so near Sunreturn, and at the Sea-Guild they told him that even fishingboats were not going out through the Armed Cliffs in the untrusty weather.

They offered him dinner at the buttery there in the

Sea-Guild; a wizard seldom has to ask for his dinner. He sat a while with those longshoremen, shipwrights, and weatherworkers, taking pleasure in their slow, sparse conversation, their grumbling Gontish speech. There was a great wish in him to stay here on Gont, and foregoing all wizardry and venture, forgetting all power and horror, to live in peace like any man on the known, dear ground of his home land. That was his wish; but his will was other. He did not stay long in the Sea-Guild, nor in the city, after he found there would be no ships out of port. He set out walking along the bay shore till he came to the first of the small villages that lie north of the City of Gont, and there he asked among the fishermen till he found one that had a boat to sell.

The fisherman was a dour old man. His boat, twelve foot long and clinker-built, was so warped and sprung as to be scarce seaworthy, yet he asked a high price for her: the spell of sea-safety for a year laid on his own boat, himself, and his son. For Gontish fishermen fear nothing, not even wizards, only the sea.

That spell of sea-safety which they set much store by in the Northern Archipelago never saved a man from storm-wind or storm-wave, but, cast by one who knows the local seas and the ways of a boat and the skills of the sailor, it weaves some daily safety about the fisherman. Ged made the charm well and honestly, working on it all that night and the next day, omitting nothing, sure and patient, though all the while his mind was strained with fear and his thoughts went on dark paths seeking to imagine how the shadow would appear to him next, and how soon, and where. When the spell was made whole and cast, he was very weary. He slept that night in the fisherman's hut in a whale-gut hammock, and got up at dawn smelling like a dried herring, and went down to the cove under Cutnorth Cliff where his new boat lay.

He pushed it into the quiet water by the landing, and water began to well softly into it at once. Stepping into the boat light as a cat Ged set straight the warped boards and rotten pegs, working both with tools and incantations, as he had used to do with Pechvarry in Low Torning. The people of the village gathered in silence, not too close, to watch his quick hands and listen to his soft voice. This job too he did well and patiently until it was done and the boat was sealed and sound. Then he set up his staff that Ogion had made him for a mast, stayed it with spells, and fixed across it a yard of sound wood. Downward from this yard he wove on the wind's loom a sail of spells, a square sail white as the snows on Gont peak above. At this the women watching sighed with envy. Then standing by the mast Ged raised up the magewind lightly. The boat moved out upon the water, turning towards the Armed Cliffs across the great bay. When the silent watching fishermen saw that leaky rowboat slip out under sail as quick and neat as a sandpiper taking wing, then they raised a cheer, grinning and stamping in the cold wind on the beach; and Ged looking back a moment saw them there cheering him on, under the dark jagged bulk of Cutnorth Cliff, above which the snowy fields of the Mountain rose up into cloud.

He sailed across the bay and out between the Armed Cliffs onto the Gontish Sea, there setting his course northwestwards to pass north of Oranéa, returning as he had come. He had no plan or strategy in this but the retracing of his course. Following his falcon-flight across the days and winds from Osskil, the shadow might wander or might come straight, there was no telling. But unless it had withdrawn again wholly into the dream-realm, it should not miss Ged coming openly, over open sea, to meet it.

On the sea he wished to meet it, if meet it he must. He was not sure why this was, yet he had a terror of meeting the thing again on dry land. Out of the sea there rise storms and monsters, but no evil powers: evil is of earth. And there is no sea, no running of river or spring, in the dark land where once Ged had gone. Death is the dry place. Though the sea itself was a danger to him in the hard weather of the season, that danger and change and instability seemed to him a defense and chance. And when he met the shadow in this final end of his folly, he thought, maybe at least he could grip the thing even as it gripped him, and drag it with the weight of his body and the weight of his own death down into the darkness of the deep sea, from which, so held, it might not rise again. So at least his death would put an end to the evil he had loosed by living.

He sailed a rough chopping sea above which clouds drooped and drifted in vast mournful veils. He raised no magewind now but used the world's wind, which blew keen from the northwest; and so long as he maintained the substance of his spell-woven sail often with a whispered word, the sail itself set and turned itself to catch the wind. Had he not used that magic he would have been hard put to keep the crank little boat on such a course, on that rough sea. On he went, and kept keen look-out on all sides. The fisherman's wife had given him two loaves of bread and a jar of water, and after some hours, when he was first in sight of Kameber Rock, the only isle between Gont and Oranéa, he ate and drank, and thought gratefully of the silent Gontishwoman who had given him the food. On past the dim glimpse of land he sailed, tacking more westerly now, in a faint dank drizzle that over land might be a light snow. There was no sound at all but the small creaking of the boat and light slap of waves on her bow. No boat or bird went by. Nothing moved but the ever-moving water and the drifting clouds, the clouds that he remembered dimly as flowing all about him as he, a falcon, flew east on this same course he now followed to the west; and he had looked down on the grey sea then as now he looked up at the grey air.

Nothing was ahead when he looked around. He stood up, chilled, weary of this gazing and peering into empty murk. "Come then," he muttered, "come on, what do you wait for, Shadow?" There was no answer, no darker motion among the dark mists and waves. Yet he knew more and more surely now that the thing was not far off, seeking blindly down his cold trail. And all at once he shouted out aloud, "I am here, I Ged the Sparrowhawk, and I summon my shadow!"

The boat creaked, the waves lisped, the wind hissed a little on the white sail. The moments went by. Still Ged waited, one hand on the yew-wood mast of his boat, staring into the icy drizzle that slowly drove in ragged lines across the sea from the north. The moments went by. Then, far off in the rain over the water, he saw the shadow coming.

It had done with the body of the Osskilian oarsman Skiorh, and not as gebbeth did it follow him through the winds and over sea. Nor did it wear that beast-shape in which he had seen it on Roke Knoll, and in his dreams. Yet it had a shape now, even in the daylight. In its pursuit of Ged and in its struggle with him on the moors it had drawn power from him, sucking it into itself: and it may be that his summoning of it, aloud in the light of day, had given to it or forced upon it some form and semblance. Certainly it had now some likeness to a man, though being shadow it cast no shadow. So it came over the sea, out of the Jaws of Enlad towards Gont, a dim ill-made thing pacing uneasy on the waves, peering down the wind as it came; and the cold rain blew through it.

Because it was half blinded by the day, and because he had called it, Ged saw it before it saw him. He knew it, as it knew him, among all beings, all shadows.

In the terrible solitude of the winter sea Ged stood and saw the thing he feared. The wind seemed to blow it farther from the boat, and the waves ran under it bewildering his eye, and ever and again it seemed closer to him. He could not tell if it moved or not. It had seen him, now. Though there was nothing in his mind but horror and fear of its touch, the cold black pain that drained his life away, yet he waited, unmoving. Then all at once speaking aloud he called the magewind strong and sudden into his white sail, and his boat leapt across the grey waves straight at the lowering thing that hung upon the wind.

In utter silence the shadow, wavering, turned and fled.

Upwind it went, northward. Upwind Ged's boat followed, shadow-speed against mage-craft, the rainy gale against them both. And the young man yelled to his boat, to the sail and the wind and the waves ahead, as a hunter yells to his hounds when the wolf runs in plain sight before them, and he brought into that spell-woven sail a wind that would have split any sail of cloth and that drove his boat over the sea like a scud of blown foam, closer always to the thing that fled.

Now the shadow turned, making a half-circle, and appearing all at once more loose and dim, less like a man more like mere smoke blowing on the wind, it doubled back and ran downwind with the gale, as if it made for Gont.

With hand and spell Ged turned his boat, and it leaped like a dolphin from the water, rolling, in that quick turn. Faster than before he followed, but the shadow grew ever fainter to his eyes. Rain, mixed with sleet and snow, came stinging across his back and his left cheek, and he could not see more than a hundred yards ahead. Before long, as the storm grew heavier, the shadow was lost to sight. Yet Ged was sure of its track as if he followed a beast's track over snow, instead of a wraith fleeing over water. Though the wind blew his way now he held the singing magewind in the sail, and flake-foam shot from the boat's blunt prow, and she slapped the water as she went.

For a long time hunted and hunter held their weird, fleet course, and the day was darkening fast. Ged knew that at the great pace he had gone these past hours he must be south of Gont, heading past it

towards Spevy or Torheven, or even past these islands out into the open Reach. He could not tell. He
did not care. He hunted, he followed, and fear ran
before him.

All at once he saw the shadow for a moment not
far from him. The world's wind had been sinking, and
the driving sleet of the storm had given way to a
chill, ragged, thickening mist. Through this mist he
glimpsed the shadow, fleeing somewhat to the right
of his course. He spoke to wind and sail and turned
the tiller and pursued, though again it was a blind
pursuit: the fog thickened fast, boiling and tattering
where it met with the spellwind, closing down all
round the boat, a featureless pallor that deadened
light and sight. Even as Ged spoke the first word of a
clearing-charm, he saw the shadow again, still to the
right of his course but very near, and going slowly.
The fog blew through the faceless vagueness of its
head, yet it was shaped like a man, only deformed
and changing, like a man's shadow. Ged veered the
boat once more, thinking he had run his enemy to
ground: in that instant it vanished, and it was his
boat that ran aground, smashing up on shoal rocks
that the blowing mist had hidden from his sight. He
was pitched nearly out, but grabbed hold on the
mast-staff before the next breaker struck. This was a
great wave, which threw the little boat up out of
water and brought her down on a rock, as a man
might lift up and crush a snail's shell.

Stout and wizardly was the staff Ogion had shaped.
It did not break, and buoyant as a dry log it rode the
water. Still grasping it Ged was pulled back as the
breakers streamed back from the shoal, so that he was
in deep water and saved, till the next wave, from battering on the rocks. Salt-blinded and choked, he tried
to keep his head up and to fight the enormous pull of
the sea. There was sand beach a little aside of the
rocks, he glimpsed this a couple of times as he tried
to swim free of the rising of the next breaker. With
all his strength and with the staff's power aiding him

he struggled to make for that beach. He got no
nearer. The surge and recoil of the swells tossed him
back and forth like a rag, and the cold of the deep
sea drew warmth fast from his body, weakening him
till he could not move his arms. He had lost sight of
rocks and beach alike, and did not know what way he
faced. There was only a tumult of water around him,
under him, over him, blinding him, strangling him,
drowning him.

A wave swelling in under the ragged fog took him
and rolled him over and over and flung him up like a
stick of driftwood on the sand.

There he lay. He still clutched the yew-wood staff
with both hands. Lesser waves dragged at him, trying
to tug him back down the sand in their outgoing
rush, and the mist parted and closed above him, and
later a sleety rain beat on him.

After a long time he moved. He got up on hands
and knees, and began slowly crawling up the beach,
away from the water's edge. It was black night now,
but he whispered to the staff, and a little werelight
clung about it. With this to guide him he struggled
forward, little by little, up toward the dunes. He was
so beaten and broken and cold that this crawling
through the wet sand in the whistling, sea-thundering
dark was the hardest thing he had ever had to do.
And once or twice it seemed to him that the great
noise of the sea and the wind all died away and the
wet sand turned to dust under his hands, and he felt
the unmoving gaze of strange stars on his back: but
he did not lift his head, and he crawled on, and after
a while he heard his own gasping breath, and felt the
bitter wind beat the rain against his face.

The moving brought a little warmth back into him
at last, and after he had crept up into the dunes,
where the gusts of rainy wind came less hard, he
managed to get up on his feet. He spoke a stronger
light out of the staff, for the world was utterly black,
and then leaning on the staff he went on, stumbling
and halting, half a mile or so inland. Then on the rise

of a dune he heard the sea, louder again, not behind him but in front: the dunes sloped down again to another shore. This was no island he was on but a mere reef, a bit of sand in the midst of the ocean.

He was too worn out to despair, but he gave a kind of sob and stood there, bewildered, leaning on his staff, for a long time. Then doggedly he turned to the left, so the wind would be at his back at least, and shuffled down the high dune, seeking some hollow among the ice-rimed, bowing sea-grass where he could have a little shelter. As he held up the staff to see what lay before him, he caught a dull gleam at the farthest edge of the circle of werelight: a wall of rain-wet wood.

It was a hut or shed, small and rickety as if a child had built it. Ged knocked on the low door with his staff. It remained shut. Ged pushed it open and entered, stooping nearly double to do so. He could not stand up straight inside the hut. Coals lay red in the firepit, and by their dim glow Ged saw a man with white, long hair, who crouched in terror against the far wall, and another, man or woman he could not tell, peering from a heap of rags or hides on the floor.

"I won't hurt you," Ged whispered.

They said nothing. He looked from one to the other. Their eyes were blank with terror. When he laid down his staff, the one under the pile of rags hid whimpering. Ged took off his cloak that was heavy with water and ice, stripped naked and huddled over the firepit. "Give me something to wrap myself in," he said. He was hoarse, and could hardly speak for the chattering of his teeth and the long shudders that shook him. If they heard him, neither of the old ones answered. He reached out and took a rag from the bed-heap—a goat-hide, it might have been years ago, but it was now all tatters and black grease. The one under the bed-heap moaned with fear, but Ged paid no heed. He rubbed himself dry and then whispered, "Have you wood? Build up the fire a little, old man. I come to you in need, I mean you no harm."

The old man did not move, watching him in a stupor of fear.

"Do you understand me? Do you speak no Hardic?" Ged paused, and then asked, "Kargad?"

At that word, the old man nodded all at once, one nod, like a sad old puppet on strings. But as it was the only word Ged knew of the Kargish language, it was the end of their conversation. He found wood piled by one wall, built up the fire himself, and then with gestures asked for water, for swallowing seawater had sickened him and now he was parched with thirst. Cringing, the old man pointed to a great shell that held water, and pushed towards the fire another shell in which were strips of smoke-dried fish. So, cross-legged close by the fire, Ged drank, and ate a little, and as some strength and sense began to come back into him, he wondered where he was. Even with the magewind he could not have sailed clear to the Kargad Lands. This islet must be out in the Reach, east of Gont but still west of Karego-At. It seemed strange that people dwelt on so small and forlorn a place, a mere sand-bar; maybe they were castaways; but he was too weary to puzzle his head about them then.

He kept turning his cloak to the heat. The silvery pellawi-fur dried fast, and as soon as the wool of the facing was at least warm, if not dry, he wrapped himself in it and stretched out by the firepit. "Go to sleep, poor folk," he said to his silent hosts, and laid his head down on the floor of sand, and slept.

Three nights he spent on the nameless isle, for the first morning when he woke he was sore in every muscle and feverish and sick. He lay like a log of driftwood in the hut by the firepit all that day and night. The next morning he woke still stiff and sore, but recovered. He put back on his salt-crusted clothes, for there was not enough water to wash them, and going out into the grey windy morning looked over this place whereto the shadow had tricked him.

It was a rocky sand-bar a mile wide at its widest
and a little longer than that, fringed all about with
shoals and rocks. No tree or bush grew on it, no plant
but the bowing sea-grass. The hut stood in a hollow
of the dunes, and the old man and woman lived there
alone in the utter desolation of the empty sea. The
hut was built, or piled up rather, of driftwood planks
and branches. Their water came from a little brackish
well beside the hut; their food was fish and shellfish,
fresh or dried, and rockweed. The tattered hides in
the hut, and a little store of bone needles and fish-
hooks, and the sinew for fishlines and firedrill, came
not from goats as Ged had thought at first, but from
spotted seal; and indeed this was the kind of place
where the seal will go to raise their pups in summer.
But no one else comes to such a place. The old ones
feared Ged not because they thought him a spirit,
and not because he was a wizard, but only because
he was a man. They had forgotten that there were
other people in the world.

The old man's sullen dread never lessened. When
he thought Ged was coming close enough to touch
him, he would hobble away, peering back with a
scowl around his bush of dirty white hair. At first the
old woman had whimpered and hidden under her
rag-pile whenever Ged moved, but as he had lain
dozing feverishly in the dark hut, he saw her squat-
ting to stare at him with a strange, dull, yearning
look; and after a while she had brought him water to
drink. When he sat up to take the shell from her she
was scared and dropped it, spilling all the water, and
then she wept, and wiped her eyes with her long
whitish-grey hair.

Now she watched him as he worked down on the
beach, shaping driftwood and planks from his boat
that had washed ashore into a new boat, using the
old man's crude stone adze and a binding-spell. This
was neither a repair nor a boat-building, for he had
not enough proper wood, and must supply all his
wants with pure wizardry. Yet the old woman did not

watch his marvellous work so much as she watched
him, with that same craving look in her eyes. After a
while she went off, and came back presently with a
gift: a handful of mussels she had gathered on the
rocks. Ged ate them as she gave them to him, sea-wet
and raw, and thanked her. Seeming to gain courage,
she went to the hut and came back with something
again in her hands, a bundle wrapped up in a rag.
Timidly, watching his face all the while, she un-
wrapped the thing and held it up for him to see.

It was a little child's dress of silk brocade stiff with
seed-pearls, stained with salt, yellow with years. On
the small bodice the pearls were worked in a shape
Ged knew: the double arrow of the God-Brothers of
the Kargad Empire, surmounted by a king's crown.

The old woman, wrinkled, dirty, clothed in an ill-
sewn sack of sealskin, pointed at the little silken dress
and at herself, and smiled: a sweet, unmeaning smile,
like a baby's. From some hidingplace sewn in the
skirt of the dress she took a small object, and this was
held out to Ged. It was a bit of dark metal, a piece of
broken jewelry perhaps, the half-circle of a broken
ring. Ged looked at it, but she gestured that he take
it, and was not satisfied until he took it; then she nodded and smiled again; she had made him a present.
But the dress she wrapped up carefully in its greasy
rag-coverings, and she shuffled back to the hut to
hide the lovely thing away.

Ged put the broken ring into his tunic-pocket with
almost the same care, for his heart was full of pity.
He guessed now that these two might be children of
some royal house of the Kargad Empire; a tyrant or
usurper who feared to shed kingly blood had sent
them to be cast away, to live or die, on an uncharted
islet far from Karego-At. One had been a boy of eight
or ten, maybe, and the other a stout baby princess in
a dress of silk and pearls; and they had lived, and
lived on alone, forty years, fifty years, on a rock in
the ocean, prince and princess of Desolation.

But the truth of this guess he did not learn until,

years later, the quest of the Ring of Erreth-Akbe led
him to the Kargad Lands, and to the Tombs of Atuan.

His third night on the isle lightened to a calm, pale
sunrise. It was the day of Sunreturn, the shortest day
of the year. His little boat of wood and magic, scraps
and spells, was ready. He had tried to tell the old
ones that he would take them to any land, Gont or
Spevy or the Torikles; he would have left them even
on some lonely shore of Karego-At, had they asked it
of him, though Kargish waters were no safe place for
an Archipelagan to venture. But they would not leave
their barren isle. The old woman seemed not to understand what he meant with his gestures and quiet
words; the old man did understand, and refused. All
his memory of other lands and other men was a
child's nightmare of blood and giants and screaming:
Ged could see that in his face, as he shook his head
and shook his head.

So Ged that morning filled up a sealskin pouch
with water at the well, and since he could not thank
the old ones for their fire and food, and had no
present for the old woman as he would have liked, he
did what he could, and set a charm on that salty un-
reliable spring. The water rose up through the sand
as sweet and clear as any mountain spring in the
heights of Gont, nor did it ever fail. Because of it,
that place of dunes and rocks is charted now and
bears a name; sailors call it Springwater Isle. But the
hut is gone, and the storms of many winters have left
no sign of the two who lived out their lives there and
died alone.

They kept hidden in the hut, as if they feared to
watch, when Ged ran his boat out from the sandy
south end of the isle. He let the world's wind, steady
from the north, fill his sail of spellcloth, and went
speedily forth over the sea.

Now this sea-quest of Ged's was a strange matter,
for as he well knew, he was a hunter who knew neither what the thing was that he hunted, nor where in

all Earthsea it might be. He must hunt it by guess, by
hunch, by luck, even as it had hunted him. Each was
blind to the other's being, Ged as baffled by impalpa-
ble shadows as the shadow was baffled by daylight
and by solid things. One certainty only Ged had: that
he was indeed the hunter now and not the hunted.
For the shadow, having tricked him onto the rocks,
might have had him at its mercy all the while he lay
half-dead on the shore and blundered in darkness in
the stormy dunes; but it had not waited for that
chance. It had tricked him and fled away at once, not
daring now to face him. In this he saw that Ogion
had been right: the shadow could not draw on his
power, so long as he was turned against it. So he
must keep against it, keep after it, though its track
was cold across these wide seas, and he had nothing
at all to guide him but the luck of the world's wind
blowing southward, and a dim guess or notion in his
mind that south or east was the right way to follow.

Before nightfall he saw away off on his left hand
the long, faint shoreline of a great land, which must
be Karego-At. He was in the very sea-roads of those
white barbaric folk. He kept a sharp watch out for
any Kargish longship or galley; and he remembered,
as he sailed through red evening, that morning of his
boyhood in Ten Alders village, the plumed warriors,
the fire, the mist. And thinking of that day he saw all
at once, with a qualm at his heart, how the shadow
had tricked him with his own trick, bringing that mist
about him on the sea as if bringing it out of his own
past, blinding him to danger and fooling him to his
death.

He kept his course to the southeast, and the land
sank out of sight as night came over the eastern edge
of the world. The hollows of the waves all were full
of darkness while the crests shone yet with a clear
ruddy reflection of the west. Ged sang aloud the Winter Carol, and such cantos of the *Deed of the Young
King* as he remembered, for those songs are sung at
the Festival of Sunreturn. His voice was clear, but it

fell to nothing in the vast silence of the sea. Darkness came quickly, and the winter stars.

All that longest night of the year he waked, watching the stars rise upon his left hand and wheel overhead and sink into far black waters on the right, while always the long wind of winter bore him southward over an unseen sea. He could sleep for only a moment now and then, with a sharp awakening. This boat he sailed was in truth no boat but a thing more than half charm and sorcery, and the rest of it mere planks and driftwood which, if he let slack the shaping-spells and the binding-spell upon them, would soon enough lapse and scatter and go drifting off as a little flotsam on the waves. The sail too, woven of magic and the air, would not long stay against the wind if he slept, but would turn to a puff of wind itself. Ged's spells were cogent and potent, but when the matter on which such spells works is small, the power that keeps them working must be renewed from moment to moment: so he slept not that night. He would have gone easier and swifter as falcon or dolphin, but Ogion had advised him not to change his shape, and he knew the value of Ogion's advice. So he sailed southward under the west-going stars, and the long night passed slowly, until the first day of the new year brightened all the sea.

Soon after the sun rose he saw land ahead, but he was making little way towards it. The world's wind had dropped with daybreak. He raised a light mage-wind into his sail, to drive him towards that land. At the sight of it, fear had come into him again, the sinking dread that urged him to turn away, to run away. And he followed that fear as a hunter follows the signs, the broad, blunt, clawed tracks of the bear, that may at any moment turn on him from the thickets. For he was close now: he knew it.

It was a queer-looking land that loomed up over the sea as he drew nearer and nearer. What had from afar seemed to be one sheer mountainwall, was split into several long steep ridges, separate isles perhaps, between which the sea ran in narrow sounds or channels. Ged had pored over many charts and maps in the Tower of the Master Namer on Roke, but those had been mostly of the Archipelago and the inner seas. He was out in the East Reach now, and did not know what this island might be. Nor had he much thought for that. It was fear that lay ahead of him, that lurked hiding from him or waiting for him among the slopes and forests of the island, and straight for it he steered.

Now the dark forest-crowned cliffs gloomed and towered high over his boat, and spray from the waves that broke against the rocky headlands blew spattering against his sail, as the magewind bore him between two great capes into a sound, a sea-lane that ran on before him deep into the island, no wider than the length of two galleys. The sea, confined, was restless and fretted at the steep shores. There were no beaches, for the cliffs dropped straight down into the water that lay darkened by the cold reflection of their heights. It was windless, and very silent.

The shadow had tricked him out onto the moors in Osskil, and tricked him in the mist onto the rocks, and now would there be a third trick? Had he driven the thing here, or had it drawn him here, into a trap? He did not know. He knew only the torment of dread, and the certainty that he must go ahead and do what he had set out to do: hunt down the evil, follow his terror to its source. Very cautiously he steered, watching before him and behind him and up and down the cliffs on either hand. He had left the sunlight of the new day behind him on the open sea. All was dark here. The opening between the headlands seemed a remote, bright gateway when he glanced back. The cliffs loomed higher and ever higher overhead as he approached the mountain-root from which they sprang, and the lane of water grew narrower. He peered ahead into the dark cleft, and left and right up the great, cavern-pocked, boulder-tumbled slopes where trees crouched with their roots half in air. Nothing moved. Now he was coming to the end of the inlet, a high blank wrinkled mass of rock against which, narrowed to the width of a little creek, the last sea-waves lapped feebly. Fallen boulders and rotten trunks and the roots of gnarled trees left only a tight way to steer. A trap: a dark trap under the roots of the silent mountain, and he was in the trap. Nothing moved before him or above him. All was deathly still. He could go no further.

He turned the boat around, working her carefully round with spell and with makeshift oar lest she knock up against the underwater rocks or be entangled in the outreaching roots and branches, till she faced outward again; and he was about to raise up a wind to take him back as he had come, when suddenly the words of the spell froze on his lips, and his heart went cold within him. He looked back over his shoulder. The shadow stood behind him in the boat.

Had he lost one instant, he had been lost; but he was ready, and lunged to seize and hold the thing which wavered and trembled there within arm's reach. No wizardry would serve him now, but only his own flesh, his life itself, against the unliving. He spoke no word, but attacked, and the boat plunged and pitched from his sudden turn and lunge. And a pain ran up his arms into his breast, taking away his breath, and an icy cold filled him, and he was blinded: yet in his hands that seized the shadow there was nothing—darkness, air.

He stumbled forward, catching the mast to stay his fall, and light came shooting back into his eyes. He saw the shadow shudder away from him and shrink together, then stretch hugely up over him, over the sail, for an instant. Then like black smoke on the wind it recoiled and fled, formless, down the water towards the bright gate between the cliffs.

Ged sank to his knees. The little spell-patched boat pitched again, rocked itself to stillness, drifting on the uneasy waves. He crouched in it, numb, unthinking, struggling to draw breath, until at last cold water welling under his hands warned him that he must see to his boat, for the spells binding it were growing weak. He stood up, holding onto the staff that made the mast, and rewove the binding-spell as best he could. He was chilled and weary; his hands and arms ached sorely, and there was no power in him. He wished he might lie down there in that dark place where sea and mountain met and sleep, sleep on the restless rocking water.

He could not tell if this weariness were a sorcery laid on him by the shadow as it fled, or came of the bitter coldness of its touch, or was from mere hunger and want of sleep and expense of strength; but he struggled against it, forcing himself to raise up a light magewind into the sail and follow down the dark sea-way where the shadow had fled.

All terror was gone. All joy was gone. It was a chase no longer. He was neither hunted nor hunter, now. For the third time they had met and touched: he had of his own will turned to the shadow, seeking to hold it with living hands. He had not held it, but he had forged between them a bond, a link that had no breaking-point. There was no need to hunt the thing down, to track it, nor would its flight avail it. Neither could escape. When they had come to the time and place for their last meeting, they would meet.

But until that time, and elsewhere than that place, there would never be any rest or peace for Ged, day or night, on earth or sea. He knew now, and the knowledge was hard, that his task had never been to undo what he had done, but to finish what he had begun.

He sailed out from between the dark cliffs, and on the sea was broad, bright morning, with a fair wind blowing from the north.

He drank what water he had left in the sealskin pouch, and steered around the westernmost headland until he came into a wide strait between it and a second island lying to the west. Then he knew the place, calling to mind sea-charts of the East Reach. These were the Hands, a pair of lonely isles that reach their mountain-fingers northward toward the Kargad Lands. He sailed on between the two, and as the afternoon darkened with storm-clouds coming up from the north he came to shore, on the southern coast of the west isle. He had seen there was a little village there, above the beach where a stream came tumbling down to the sea, and he cared little what welcome he got if he could have water, fire's warmth, and sleep.

The villagers were rough shy people, awed by a wizard's staff, wary of a strange face, but hospitable to one who came alone, over sea, before a storm. They gave him meat and drink in plenty, and the comfort of firelight and the comfort of human voices speaking his own Hardic tongue, and last and best they gave him hot water to wash the cold and saltness of the sea from him, and a bed where he could sleep.

# 9 Iffish

Ged spent three days in that village of the West Hand, recovering himself, and making ready a boat built not of spells and sea-wrack but of sound wood well pegged and caulked, with a stout mast and sail of her own, that he might sail easily and sleep when he needed. Like most boats of the North and the Reaches she was clinker-built, with planks overlapped and clenched one upon the other for strength in the high seas; every part of her was sturdy and well-made. Ged reinforced her wood with deep-inwoven charms, for he thought he might go far in that boat. She was built to carry two or three men, and the old man who owned her said that he and his brothers had been through high seas and foul weather with her and she had ridden all gallantly.

Unlike the shrewd fisherman of Gont, this old man, for fear and wonder of his wizardry, would have given the boat to Ged. But Ged paid him for it in sorcerers' kind, healing his eyes of the cataracts that were in the way of blinding him. Then the old man, rejoicing, said to him, "We called the boat *Sanderling,* but do you call her *Lookfar*, and paint eyes aside her prow, and my thanks will look out of that blind wood for you and keep you from rock and reef. For I had forgotten how much light there is in the world, till you gave it back to me."

Other works Ged also did in his days in that village under the steep forests of the Hand, as his power came back into him. These were such people as he had known as a boy in the Northward Vale of Gont, though poorer even than those. With them he was at home, as he would never be in the courts of the wealthy, and he knew their bitter wants without having to ask. So he laid charms of heal and ward on children who were lame or sickly, and spells of increase on the villagers' scrawny flocks of goats and sheep; he set the rune Simn on the spindles and looms, the boat's oars and tools of bronze and stone they brought him, that these might do their work well; and the rune Pirr he wrote on the rooftrees of the huts, which protects the house and its folk from fire, wind, and madness.

When his boat *Lookfar* was ready and well stocked with water and dried fish, he stayed yet one more day in the village, to teach to their young chanter the Deed of Morred and the Havnorian Lay. Very seldom did any Archipelagan ship touch at the Hands: songs made a hundred years ago were news to those villagers, and they craved to hear of heroes. Had Ged been free of what was laid on him he would gladly have stayed there a week or a month to sing them what he knew, that the great songs might be known on a new isle. But he was not free, and the next morning he set sail, going straight south over the wide seas of the Reach. For southward the shadow had gone. He need cast no finding-charm to know this: he knew it, as certainly as if a fine unreeling cord bound him and it together, no matter what miles and seas and lands might lie between. So he went certain, unhurried, and unhopeful on the way he

must go, and the wind of winter bore him to the
south.

He sailed a day and a night over the lonesome sea,
and on the second day he came to a small isle, which
they told him was called Vemish. The people in the
little port looked at him askance, and soon their sorcerer came hurrying. He looked hard at Ged, and
then he bowed, and said in a voice that was both
pompous and wheedling, "Lord Wizard! forgive my
temerity, and honor us by accepting of us anything
you may need for your voyage—food, drink, sailcloth,
rope,—my daughter is fetching to your boat at this
moment a brace of fresh-roasted hens—I think it
prudent, however, that you continue on your way
from here as soon as it meets your convenience to do
so. The people are in some dismay. For not long ago,
the day before yesterday, a person was seen crossing
our humble isle afoot from north to south, and no
boat was seen to come with him aboard it nor no boat
was seen to leave with him aboard it, and it did not
seem that he cast any shadow. Those who saw this
person tell me that he bore some likeness to yourself."

At that, Ged bowed his own head, and turned and
went back to the docks of Vemish and sailed out, not
looking back. There was no profit in frightening the
islanders or making an enemy of their sorcerer. He
would rather sleep at sea again, and think over this
news the sorcerer had told him, for he was sorely
puzzled by it.

The day ended, and the night passed with cold rain
whispering over the sea all through the dark hours,
and a grey dawn. Still the mild north wind carried
*Lookfar* on. After noon the rain and mist blew off,
and the sun shone from time to time; and late in the
day Ged saw right athwart his course the low blue
hills of a great island, brightened by that drifting
winter sunlight. The smoke of hearthfires lingered
blue over the slate roofs of little towns among those
hills, a pleasant sight in the vast sameness of the sea.

Ged followed a fishing-fleet in to their port, and

going up the streets of the town in the golden winter evening he found an inn called *The Harrekki,* where firelight and ale and roast ribs of mutton warmed him body and soul. At the tables of the inn there were a couple of other voyagers, traders of the East Reach, but most of the men were townsfolk come there for good ale, news, and conversation. They were not rough timid people like the fisher-folk of the Hands, but true townsmen, alert and sedate. Surely they knew Ged for a wizard, but nothing at all was said of it, except that the innkeeper in talking (and he was a talkative man) mentioned that this town, Ismay, was fortunate in sharing with other towns of the island the inestimable treasure of an accomplished wizard trained at the School on Roke, who had been given his staff by the Archmage himself, and who, though out of town at the moment, dwelt in his ancestral home right in Ismay itself, which, therefore, stood in no need of any other practitioner of the High Arts. "As they say, *two staffs in one town must come to blows,* isn't it so, Sir?" said the innkeeper, smiling and full of cheer. So Ged was informed that as journeyman-wizard, one seeking a livelihood from sorcery, he was not wanted here. Thus he had got a blunt dismissal from Vemish and a bland one from Ismay, and he wondered at what he had been told about the kindly ways of the East Reach. This isle was Iffish, where his friend Vetch had been born. It did not seem so hospitable a place as Vetch had said.

And yet he saw that they were, indeed, kindly faces enough. It was only that they sensed what he knew to be true: that he was set apart from them, cut off from them, that he bore a doom upon him and followed after a dark thing. He was like a cold wind blowing through the firelit room, like a black bird carried by on a storm from foreign lands. The sooner he went on, taking his evil destiny with him, the better for these folk.

"I am on quest," he said to the innkeeper. "I will be here only a night or two." His tone was bleak. The

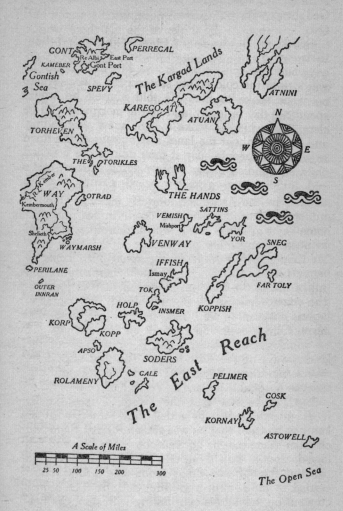

CONT
PERREGAL
KAMEBER    Re Albi    East Port
Gontish    Gont Port
Sea    SPEVY
The Kargad Lands
ATNINI
KAREGO-AT
ATUAN
TORHEVEN
N
THE    TORIKLES
W    E
S
THE HANDS
K ember    VEMISH    SATTINS
WAY    OTRAD    Mishport
Kembermouth    YOR
VENWAY
Shelieth
WAYMARSH    SNEG
IFFISH
PERILANE    Ismay    FAR TOLY
TOK
OUTER    INSMER    KOPPISH
INNRAN    HOLP
KORP    The East Reach
KOPP
APSO
SODERS
ROLAMENY    GALE    PELIMER
The    COSK
KORNAY
ASTOWELL

A Scale of Miles

25  50    100    150    200    300

The Open Sea

innkeeper, with a glance at the great yew-staff in the corner, said nothing at all for once, but filled up Ged's cup with brown ale till the foam ran over the top.

Ged knew that he should spend only the one night in Ismay. There was no welcome for him there, or anywhere. He must go where he was bound. But he was sick of the cold empty sea and the silence where no voice spoke to him. He told himself he would spend one day in Ismay, and on the morrow go. So he slept late; when he woke a light snow was falling, and he idled about the lanes and byways of the town to watch the people busy at their doings. He watched children bundled in fur capes playing at snow-castle and building snowmen; he heard gossips chatting across the street from open doors, and watched the bronze-smith at work with a little lad red-faced and sweating to pump the long bellows-sleeves at the smelting pit; through windows lit with a dim ruddy gold from within as the short day darkened he saw women at their looms, turning a moment to speak or smile to child or husband there in the warmth within the house. Ged saw all these things from outside and apart, alone, and his heart was very heavy in him, though he would not admit to himself that he was sad. As night fell he still lingered in the streets, reluctant to go back to the inn. He heard a man and a girl talking together merrily as they came down the street past him towards the town square, and all at once he turned, for he knew the man's voice.

He followed and caught up with the pair, coming up beside them in the late twilight lit only by distant lantern-gleams. The girl stepped back, but the man stared at him and then flung up the staff he carried, holding it between them as a barrier to ward off the threat or act of evil. And that was somewhat more than Ged could bear. His voice shook a little as he said, "I thought you would know me, Vetch."

Even then Vetch hesitated for a moment.

"I do know you," he said, and lowered the staff and

took Ged's hand and hugged him round the shoulders—"I do know you! Welcome, my friend, welcome! What a sorry greeting I gave you, as if you were a ghost coming up from behind—and I have waited for you to come, and looked for you—"

"So you are the wizard they boast of in Ismay? I wondered—"

"Oh, yes, I'm their wizard; but listen, let me tell you why I didn't know you, lad. Maybe I've looked too hard for you. Three days ago—were you here three days ago, on Iffish?"

"I came yesterday."

"Three days ago, in the street in Quor, the village up there in the hills, I saw you. That is, I saw a presentment of you, or an imitation of you, or maybe simply a man who looks like you. He was ahead of me, going out of town, and he turned a bend in the road even as I saw him. I called and got no answer, I followed and found no one; nor any tracks; but the ground was frozen. It was a queer thing, and now seeing you come up out of the shadows like that I thought I was tricked again. I am sorry, Ged." He spoke Ged's true name softly, so that the girl who stood waiting a little way behind him would not hear it.

Ged also spoke low, to use his friend's true name: "No matter, Estarriol. But this is myself, and I am glad to see you. . . ."

Vetch heard, perhaps, something more than simple gladness in his voice. He had not yet let go of Ged's shoulder, and he said now, in the True Speech, "In trouble and from darkness you come, Ged, yet your coming is joy to me." Then he went on in his Reach-accented Hardic, "Come on, come home with us, we're going home, it's time. to get in out of the dark!—This is my sister, the youngest of us, prettier than I am as you see, but much less clever: Yarrow she's called. Yarrow, this is the Sparrowhawk, the best of us and my friend."

"Lord Wizard," the girl greeted him, and decor-

ously she bobbed her head and hid her eyes with her
hands to show respect, as women did in the East
Reach; her eyes when not hidden were clear, shy, and
curious. She was perhaps fourteen years old, dark like
her brother, but very slight and slender. On her
sleeve there clung, winged and taloned, a dragon no
longer than her hand.

They set off down the dusky street together, and
Ged remarked as they went along, "In Gont they say
Gontish women are brave, but I never saw a maiden
there wear a dragon for a bracelet."

This made Yarrow laugh, and she answered him
straight, "This is only a harrekki, have you no harrekki on Gont?" Then she got shy for a moment and
hid her eyes.

"No, nor no dragons. Is not the creature a dragon?"

"A little one, that lives in oak trees, and eats wasps
and worms and sparrows' eggs—it grows no greater
than this. Oh, Sir, my brother has told me often of
the pet you had, the wild thing, the otak—do you
have it still?"

"No. No longer."

Vetch turned to him as if with a question, but he
held his tongue and asked nothing till much later,
when the two of them sat alone over the stone firepit
of Vetch's house.

Though he was the chief wizard in the whole island of Iffish, Vetch made his home in Ismay, this
small town where he had been born, living with his
youngest brother and sister. His father had been a
sea-trader of some means, and the house was spacious
and strong-beamed, with much homely wealth of pot-
tery and fine weaving and vessels of bronze and brass
on carven shelves and chests. A great Taonian harp
stood in one corner of the main room, and Yarrow's
tapestry-loom in another, its tall frame inlaid with
ivory. There Vetch for all his plain quiet ways was
both a powerful wizard and a lord in his own house.
There were a couple of old servants, prospering along
with the house, and the brother, a cheerful lad, and

Yarrow, quick and silent as a little fish, who served the two friends their supper and ate with them, listening to their talk, and afterwards slipped off to her own room. All things here were well-founded, peaceful, and assured; and Ged looking about him at the firelit room said, "This is how a man should live," and sighed.

"Well, it's one good way," said Vetch. "There are others. Now, lad, tell me if you can what things have come to you and gone from you since we last spoke, two years ago. And tell me what journey you are on, since I see well that you won't stay long with us this time."

Ged told him, and when he was done Vetch sat pondering for a long while. Then he said, "I'll go with you, Ged."

"No."

"I think I will."

"No, Estarriol. This is no task or bane of yours. I began this evil course alone, I will finish it alone, I do not want any other to suffer from it—you least of all, you who tried to keep my hand from the evil act in the very beginning, Estarriol—"

"Pride was ever your mind's master," his friend said smiling, as if they talked of a matter of small concern to either. "Now think: it is your quest, assuredly, but if the quest fail, should there not be another there who might bear warning to the Archipelago? For the shadow would be a fearful power then. And if you defeat the thing, should there not be another there who will tell of it in the Archipelago, that the Deed may be known and sung? I know I can be of no use to you; yet I think I should go with you."

So entreated Ged could not deny his friend, but he said, "I should not have stayed this day here. I knew it, but I stayed."

"Wizards do not meet by chance, lad," said Vetch. "And after all, as you said yourself, I was with you at the beginning of your journey. It is right that I

should follow you to its end." He put new wood on
the fire, and they sat gazing into the flames a while.

"There is one I have not heard of since that night
on Roke Knoll, and I had no heart to ask any at the
School of him: Jasper I mean."

"He never won his staff. He left Roke that same
summer, and went to the Island of O to be sorcerer in
the Lord's household at O-tokne. I know no more of
him than that."

Again they were silent, watching the fire and en-
joying (since it was a bitter night) the warmth on
their legs and faces as they sat on the broad coping
of the firepit, their feet almost among the coals.

Ged said at last, speaking low, "There is a thing
that I fear, Estarriol. I fear it more if you are with me
when I go. There in the Hands in the dead end of the
inlet I turned upon the shadow, it was within my
hands' reach, and I seized it—I tried to seize it. And
there was nothing I could hold. I could not defeat it.
It fled, I followed. But that may happen again, and
yet again. I have no power over the thing. There may
be neither death nor triumph to end this quest; nothing to sing of; no end. It may be I must spend my life
running from sea to sea and land to land on an endless vain venture, a shadow-quest."

"Avert!" said Vetch, turning his left hand in the
gesture that turns aside the ill chance spoken of. For
all his somber thoughts this made Ged grin a little,
for it is rather a child's charm than a wizard's; there
was always such village innocence in Vetch. Yet also
he was keen, shrewd, direct to the center of a thing.
He said now, "That is a grim thought and I trust a
false one. I guess rather that what I saw begin, I may
see end. Somehow you will learn its nature, its being,
what it is, and so hold and bind and vanquish it.
Though that is a hard question: what is it. . . . There
is a thing that worries me, I do not understand it. It
seems the shadow now goes in your shape, or a kind
of likeness of you at least, as they saw it on Vemish

and as I saw it here in Iffish. How may that be, and why, and why did it never do so in the Archipelago?"

"They say, *Rules change in the Reaches.*"

"Aye, a true saying, I can tell you. There are good spells I learned on Roke that have no power here, or go all awry; and also there are spells worked here I never learned on Roke. Every land has its own powers, and the farther one goes from the Inner Lands, the less one can guess about those powers and their governance. But I do not think it is only that which works this change in the shadow."

"Nor do I. I think that, when I ceased to flee from it and turned against it, that turning of my will upon it gave it shape and form, even though the same act prevented it from taking my strength from me. All my acts have their echo in it; it is my creature."

"In Osskil it named you, and so stopped any wizardry you might have used against it. Why did it not do so again, there in the Hands?"

"I do not know. Perhaps it is only from my weakness that it draws the strength to speak. Almost with my own tongue it speaks: for how did it know my name? How did it know my name? I have racked my brains on that over all the seas since I left Gont, and I cannot see the answer. Maybe it cannot speak at all in its own form or formlessness, but only with borrowed tongue, as a gebbeth. I do not know."

"Then you must beware meeting it in gebbeth-form a second time."

"I think," Ged replied, stretching out his hands to the red coals as if he felt an inward chill, "I think I will not. It is bound to me now as I am to it. It cannot get so far free of me as to seize any other man and empty him of will and being, as it did Skiorh. It can possess me. If ever I weaken again, and try to escape from it, to break the bond, it will possess me. And yet, when I held it with all the strength I had, it became mere vapor, and escaped from me.... And so it will again, and yet it cannot really escape, for I can always find it. I am bound to the foul cruel thing, and will be forever, unless I can learn the word that masters it: its name."

Brooding his friend asked, "Are there names in the dark realms?"

"Gensher the Archmage said there are not. My master Ogion said otherwise."

"*Infinite are the arguments of mages,*" Vetch quoted, with a smile that was somewhat grim.

"She who served the Old Power on Osskil swore that the Stone would tell me the shadow's name, but that I count for little. However there was also a dragon, who offered to trade that name for his own, to be rid of me; and I have thought that, where mages argue, dragons may be wise."

"Wise, but unkind. But what dragon is this? You did not tell me you had been talking with dragons since I saw you last."

They talked together late that night, and though always they came back to the bitter matter of what lay before Ged, yet their pleasure in being together over-rode all; for the love between them was strong and steadfast, unshaken by time or chance. In the morning Ged woke beneath his friend's roof, and while he was still drowsy he felt such wellbeing as if he were in some place wholly defended from evil and harm. All day long a little of this dream-peace clung to his thoughts, and he took it, not as a good omen, but as a gift. It seemed likely to him that leaving this house he would leave the last haven he was to know, and so while the short dream lasted he would be happy in it.

Having affairs he must see to before he left Iffish, Vetch went off to other villages of the island with the lad who served him as prentice-sorcerer. Ged stayed with Yarrow and her brother, called Murre, who was between her and Vetch in age. He seemed not much more than a boy, for there was no gift or scourge of mage-power in him, and he had never been anywhere but Iffish, Tok, and Holp, and his life was easy and untroubled. Ged watched him with wonder and some envy, and exactly so he watched Ged: to each it seemed very queer that the other, so different, yet was his own age, nineteen years. Ged marvelled how one who had lived nineteen years could be so care-free. Admiring Murre's comely, cheerful face he felt himself to be all lank and harsh, never guessing that Murre envied him even the scars that scored his face, and thought them the track of a dragon's claws and the very rune and sign of a hero.

The two young men were thus somewhat shy with each other, but as for Yarrow she soon lost her awe of Ged, being in her own house and mistress of it. He was very gentle with her, and many were the ques-tions she asked of him, for Vetch, she said, would never tell her anything. She kept busy those two days making dry wheatcakes for the voyagers to carry, and wrapping up dried fish and meat and other such provender to stock their boat, until Ged told her to stop, for he did not plan to sail clear to Selidor with-out a halt.

"Where is Selidor?"

"Very far out in the Western Reach, where dragons are as common as mice."

"Best stay in the East then, our dragons are as small as mice. There's your meat, then; you're sure that's enough? Listen, I don't understand: you and my brother both are mighty wizards, you wave your hand and mutter and the thing is done. Why do you get hungry, then? When it comes suppertime at sea, why not say, *Meat-pie!* and the meat-pie appears, and you eat it?"

"Well, we could do so. But we don't much wish to eat our words, as they say. *Meat-pie!* is only a word, after all. . . . We can make it odorous, and savorous, and even filling, but it remains a word. It fools the stomach and gives no strength to the hungry man."

"Wizards, then, are not cooks," said Murre, who was sitting across the kitchen hearth from Ged, carv-ing a box-lid of fine wood; he was a woodworker by trade, though not a very zealous one.

"Nor are cooks wizards, alas," said Yarrow on her

knees to see if the last batch of cakes baking on the hearth-bricks was getting brown. "But I still don't understand, Sparrowhawk. I have seen my brother, and even his prentice, make light in a dark place only by saying one word: and the light shines, it is bright, not a word but a light you can see your way by!"

"Aye," Ged answered. "Light is a power. A great power, by which we exist, but which exists beyond our needs, in itself. Sunlight and starlight are time, and time is light. In the sunlight, in the days and years, life is. In a dark place life may call upon the light, naming it.—But usually when you see a wizard name or call upon some thing, some object to appear, that is not the same, he calls upon no power greater than himself, and what appears is an illusion only. To summon a thing that is not there at all, to call it by speaking its true name, that is a great mastery, not lightly used. Not for mere hunger's sake. Yarrow, your little dragon has stolen a cake."

Yarrow had listened so hard, gazing at Ged as he spoke, that she had not seen the harrekki scuttle down from its warm perch on the kettle-hook over the hearth and seize a wheatcake bigger than itself. She took the small scaly creature on her knee and fed it bits and crumbs, while she pondered what Ged had told her.

"So then you would not summon up a real meat-pie lest you disturb what my brother is always talking about—I forget its name—"

"Equilibrium," Ged replied soberly, for she was very serious.

"Yes. But, when you were shipwrecked, you sailed from the place in a boat woven mostly of spells, and it didn't leak water. Was it illusion?"

"Well, partly it was illusion, because I am uneasy seeing the sea through great holes in my boat, so I patched them for the looks of the thing. But the strength of the boat was not illusion, nor summoning, but made with another kind of art, a binding-spell. The wood was bound as one whole, one entire thing, a boat. What is a boat but a thing that doesn't leak water?"

"I've bailed some that do," said Murre.

"Well, mine leaked, too, unless I was constantly seeing to the spell." He bent down from his corner seat and took a cake from the bricks, and juggled it in his hands. "I too have stolen a cake."

"You have burned fingers, then. And when you're starving on the waste water between the far isles you'll think of that cake and say, *Ah! had I not stolen that cake I might eat it now, alas!*—I shall eat my brother's, so he can starve with you—"

"Thus is Equilibrium maintained," Ged remarked, while she took and munched a hot, half-toasted cake; and this made her giggle and choke. But presently looking serious again she said, "I wish I could truly understand what you tell me. I am too stupid."

"Little sister," Ged said, "it is I that have no skill explaining. If we had more time—"

"We will have more time," Yarrow said. "When my brother comes back home, you will come with him, for a while at least, won't you?"

"If I can," he answered gently.

There was a little pause; and Yarrow asked, watching the harrekki climb back to its perch, "Tell me just this, if it is not a secret: what other great powers are there beside the light?"

"It is no secret. All power is one in source and end, I think. Years and distances, stars and candles, water and wind and wizardry, the craft in a man's hand and the wisdom in a tree's root: they all arise together. My name, and yours, and the true name of the sun, or a spring of water, or an unborn child, all are syllables of the great word that is very slowly spoken by the shining of the stars. There is no other power. No other name."

Staying his knife on the carved wood, Murre asked, "What of death?"

The girl listened, her shining black head bent down.

"For a word to be spoken," Ged answered slowly, "there must be silence. Before, and after." Then all at once he got up, saying, "I have no right to speak of these things. The word that was mine to say I said wrong. It is better that I keep still; I will not speak again. Maybe there is no true power but the dark." And he left the fireside and the warm kitchen, taking up his cloak and going out alone into the drizzling cold rain of winter in the streets.

"He is under a curse," Murre said, gazing somewhat fearfully after him.

"I think this voyage he is on leads him to his death," the girl said, "and he fears that, yet he goes on." She lifted her head as if she watched, through the red flame of the fire, the course of a boat that came through the seas of winter alone, and went on out into empty seas. Then her eyes filled with tears a moment, but she said nothing.

Vetch came home the next day, and took his leave of the notables of Ismay, who were most unwilling to let him go off to sea in midwinter on a mortal quest not even his own; but though they might reproach him, there was nothing at all they could do to stop him. Growing weary of old men who nagged him, he said, "I am yours, by parentage and custom and by duty undertaken towards you. I am your wizard. But it is time you recalled that, though I am a servant, I am not your servant. When I am free to come back I will come back: till then farewell."

At daybreak, as grey light welled up in the east from the sea, the two young men set forth in *Lookfar* from the harbor of Ismay, raising a brown, strong-woven sail to the north wind. On the dock Yarrow stood and watched them go, as sailor's wives and sisters stand on all the shores of all Earthsea watching their men go out on the sea, and they do not wave or call aloud, but stand still in hooded cloak of grey or brown, there on the shore that dwindles smaller and smaller from the boat while the water grows wide between.

# 10 The Open Sea

The haven now was sunk from sight and *Lookfar*'s painted eyes, wave-drenched, looked ahead on seas ever wider and more desolate. In two days and nights the companions made the crossing from Iffish to Soders Island, a hundred miles of foul weather and contrary winds. They stayed in port there only briefly, long enough to refill a waterskin, and to buy a tar-smeared sailcloth to protect some of their gear in the undecked boat from seawater and rain. They had not provided this earlier, because ordinarily a wizard looks after such small conveniences by way of spells, the very least and commonest kind of spells, and indeed it takes little more magic to freshen seawater and so save the bother of carrying fresh water. But Ged seemed most unwilling to use his craft, or to let Vetch use his. He said only, "It's better not," and his friend did not ask or argue. For as the wind first filled their sail, both had felt a heavy foreboding, cold as that winter wind. Haven, harbor, peace, safety, all that was behind. They had turned away. They went now a way in which all events were perilous, and no acts were meaningless. On the course on which they were embarked, the saying of the least spell might change chance and move the balance of power and of doom: for they went now toward the very center of that balance, toward the place where light and darkness meet. Those who travel thus say no word carelessly.

Sailing out again and coasting round the shores of Soders, where white snowfields faded up into foggy hills, Ged took the boat southward again, and now they entered waters where the great traders of the Archipelago never come, the outmost fringes of the Reach.

Vetch asked no question about their course, knowing that Ged did not choose it but went as he must go. As Soders Island grew small and pale behind them, and the waves hissed and smacked under the prow, and the great grey plain of water circled them all round clear to the edge of the sky, Ged asked, "What lands lie ahead this course?"

"Due south of Soders there are no lands at all. Southeast you go a long way and find little: Pelimer, Kornay, Gosk, and Astowell which is also called Lastland. Beyond it, the Open Sea."

"What to the southwest?"

"Rolameny, which is one of our East Reach isles, and some small islets round about it; then nothing till you enter the South Reach: Rood, and Toom, and the Isle of the Ear where men do not go."

"We may," Ged said wryly.

"I'd rather not," said Vetch—"that is a disagreeable part of the world, they say, full of bones and portents. Sailors say that there are stars to be seen from the waters by the Isle of the Ear and Far Sorr that cannot be seen anywhere else, and that have never been named."

"Aye, there was a sailor on the ship that brought me first to Roke who spoke of that. And he told tales of the Raft-Folk in the far South Reach, who never come to land but once a year, to cut the great logs for their rafts, and the rest of the year, all the days and months, they drift on the currents of ocean, out of sight of any land. I'd like to see those raft-villages."

"I would not," said Vetch grinning. "Give me land, and land-folk; the sea in its bed and I in mine. . . ."

"I wish I could have seen all the cities of the Archipelago," Ged said as he held the sail-rope, watching the wide grey wastes before them. "Havnor at the world's heart, and Éa where the myths were born, and Shelieth of the Fountains on Way; all the cities and the great lands. And the small lands, the strange lands of the Outer Reaches, them too. To sail right down the Dragons' Run, away in the west. Or to sail north into the ice-floes, clear to Hogen Land. Some say that is a land greater than all the Archipelago, and others say it is mere reefs and rocks with ice between. No one knows. I should like to see the whales in the northern seas. . . . But I cannot. I must go where I am bound to go, and turn my back on the bright shores. I was in too much haste, and now have no time left. I traded all the sunlight and the cities and the distant lands for a handful of power, for a shadow, for the dark." So, as the mage-born will, Ged made his fear and regret into a song, a brief lament, half-sung, that was not for himself alone; and his friend replying spoke the hero's words from the *Deed of Erreth-Akbe,* "O may I see the earth's bright hearth once more, the white towers of Havnor. . . ."

So they sailed on their narrow course over the wide forsaken waters. The most they saw that day was a school of silver pannies swimming south, but never a dolphin leapt nor did the flight of gull or murre or tern break the grey air. As the east darkened and the west grew red, Vetch brought out food and divided it between them and said, "Here's the last of the ale. I drink to the one who thought to put the keg aboard for thirsty men in cold weather: my sister Yarrow."

At that Ged left off his bleak thoughts and his gazing ahead over the sea, and he saluted Yarrow more earnestly, perhaps, than Vetch. The thought of her brought to his mind the sense of her wise and childish sweetness. She was not like any person he had known. (What young girl had he ever known at all? but he never thought of that.) "She is like a little fish, a minnow, that swims in a clear creek," he said, "—defenseless, yet you cannot catch her."

At this Vetch looked straight at him, smiling. "You are a mage born," he said. "Her true name is Kest." In the Old Speech, *kest* is minnow, as Ged well knew; and this pleased him to the heart. But after a while he said in a low voice, "You should not have told me her name, maybe."

But Vetch, who had not done so lightly, said, "Her name is safe with you as mine is. And, besides, you knew it without my telling you. . . ."

Red sank to ashes in the west, and ash-grey sank to black. All the sea and sky were wholly dark. Ged stretched out in the bottom of the boat to sleep, wrapped in his cloak of wool and fur. Vetch, holding the sail-rope, sang softly from the *Deed of Enlad,* where the song tells how the mage Morred the White left Havnor in his oarless longship, and coming to the island Soléa saw Elfarran in the orchards in the spring. Ged slept before the song came to the sorry end of their love, Morred's death, the ruin of Enlad, the sea-waves, vast and bitter, whelming the orchards of Soléa. Towards midnight he woke, and watched again while Vetch slept. The little boat ran sharp over choppy seas, fleeing the strong wind that leaned on her sail, running blind through the night. But the overcast had broken, and before dawn the thin moon shining between brown-edged clouds shed a weak light on the sea.

"The moon wanes to her dark," Vetch murmured, awake in the dawn, when for a while the cold wind dropped. Ged looked up at the white half-ring above the paling eastern waters, but said nothing. The dark of the moon that follows first after Sunreturn is called the Fallows, and is the contrary pole of the days of the Moon and the Long Dance in summer. It is an unlucky time for travellers and for the sick; children are not given their true name during the Fallows, and no Deeds are sung, nor swords nor edge-tools sharpened, nor oaths sworn. It is the dark axis of the year, when things done are ill done.

Three days out from Soders they came, following sea-birds and shore-wrack, to Pelimer, a small isle humped high above the high grey seas. Its people spoke Hardic, but in their own fashion, strange even to Vetch's ears. The young men came ashore there for fresh water and a respite from the sea, and at first were well received, with wonder and commotion. There was a sorcerer in the main town of the island, but he was mad. He would talk only of the great serpent that was eating at the foundations of Pelimer so that soon the island must go adrift like a boat cut from her moorings, and slide out over the edge of the world. At first he greeted the young wizards courteously, but as he talked about the serpent he began to look askance at Ged: and then he fell to railing at them there in the street, calling them spies and servants of the Sea-Snake. The Pelimerians looked dourly at them after that, since though mad he was their sorcerer. So Ged and Vetch made no long stay, but set forth again before nightfall, going always south and east.

In these days and nights of sailing Ged never spoke of the shadow, nor directly of his quest; and the nearest Vetch came to asking any question was (as they followed the same course farther and farther out and away from the known lands of Earthsea)—"Are you sure?—" To this Ged answered only, "Is the iron sure where the magnet lies?" Vetch nodded and they went on, no more being said by either. But from time to time they talked of the crafts and devices that mages of old days had used to find out the hidden name of baneful powers and beings: how Nereger of Paln had learned the Black Mage's name from overhearing the conversation of dragons, and how Morred had seen his enemy's name written by falling rain-drops in the dust of the battlefield of the Plains of Enlad. They spoke of finding-spells, and invocations, and those Answerable Questions which only the Master Patterner of Roke can ask. But often Ged would end by murmuring words which Ogion had said to him on the shoulder of Gont Mountain in an autumn long ago: "To hear, one must be silent...." And he would fall silent, and ponder, hour by hour, always watching the sea ahead of the boat's way. Sometimes it seemed to Vetch that his friend saw, across the waves and miles and grey days yet to come, the thing they followed and the dark end of their voyage.

They passed between Kornay and Gosk in foul weather, seeing neither isle in the fog and rain, and knowing they had passed them only on the next day when they saw ahead of them an isle of pinnacled cliffs above which sea-gulls wheeled in huge flocks whose mewing clamor could be heard from far over the sea. Vetch said, "That will be Astowell, from the look of it. Lastland. East and south of it the charts are empty."

"Yet they who live there may know of farther lands," Ged answered.

"Why do you say so?" Vetch asked, for Ged had spoken uneasily; and his answer to this again was halting and strange. "Not there," he said, gazing at Astowell ahead, and past it, or through it—"Not there. Not on the sea. Not on the sea but on dry land: what land? Before the springs of the open sea, beyond the sources, behind the gates of daylight—"

Then he fell silent, and when he spoke again it was in an ordinary voice, as if he had been freed from a spell or a vision, and had no clear memory of it.

The port of Astowell, a creek-mouth between rocky heights, was on the northern shore of the isle, and all the huts of the town faced north and west; it was as if the island turned its face, though from so far away, always towards Earthsea, towards mankind.

Excitement and dismay attended the arrival of

strangers, in a season when no boat had ever braved
the seas round Astowell. The women all stayed in the
wattle huts, peering out the door, hiding their children behind their skirts, drawing back fearfully into
the darkness of the huts as the strangers came up
from the beach. The men, lean fellows ill-clothed
against the cold, gathered in a solemn circle about
Vetch and Ged, and each one held a stone hand-axe
or a knife of shell. But once their fear was past they
made the strangers very welcome, and there was no
end to their questions. Seldom did any ship come to
them even from Soders or Rolameny, they having
nothing to trade for bronze or fine wares; they had
not even any wood. Their boats were coracles woven
of reed, and it was a brave sailor who would go as far
as Gosk or Kornay in such a craft. They dwelt all
alone here at the edge of all the maps. They had no
witch or sorcerer, and seemed not to recognise the
young wizards' staffs for what they were, admiring
them only for the precious stuff they were made of,
wood. Their chief or Isle-Man was very old, and he
alone of his people had ever before seen a man born
in the Archipelago. Ged, therefore, was a marvel to
them; the men brought their little sons to look at the
Archipelagan, so they might remember him when
they were old. They had never heard of Gont, only of
Havnor and Éa, and took him for a Lord of Havnor.
He did his best to answer their questions about the
white city he had never seen. But he was restless as
the evening wore on, and at last he asked the men of
the village, as they sat crowded round the firepit in
the lodgehouse in the reeking warmth of the goat-
dung and broom-faggots that were all their fuel,
"What lies eastward of your land?"

They were silent, some grinning others grim.

The old Isle-Man answered, "The sea."

"There is no land beyond?"

"This is Lastland. There is no land beyond. There
is nothing but water till world's edge."

"These are wise men, father," said a younger man,

"seafarers, voyagers. Maybe they know of a land we do not know of."

"There is no land east of this land," said the old man, and he looked long at Ged, and spoke no more to him.

The companions slept that night in the smoky warmth of the lodge. Before daylight Ged roused his friend, whispering, "Estarriol, wake. We cannot stay, we must go."

"Why so soon?" Vetch asked, full of sleep.

"Not soon—late. I have followed too slow. It has found the way to escape me, and so doom me. It must not escape me, for I must follow it however far it goes. If I lose it I am lost."

"Where do we follow it?"

"Eastward. Come. I filled the waterskins."

So they left the lodge before any in the village was awake, except a baby that cried a little in the darkness of some hut, and fell still again. By the vague starlight they found the way down to the creek-mouth, and untied *Lookfar* from the rock cairn where she had been made fast, and pushed her out into the black water. So they set out eastward from Astowell into the Open Sea, on the first day of the Fallows, before sunrise.

That day they had clear skies. The world's wind was cold and gusty from the northeast, but Ged had raised the magewind: the first act of magery he had done since he left the Isle of the Hands. They sailed very fast due eastward. The boat shuddered with the great, smoking, sunlit waves that hit her as she ran, but she went gallantly as her builder had promised, answering the magewind as true as any spell-enwoven ship of Roke.

Ged spoke not at all that morning, except to renew the power of the wind-spell or to keep a charmed strength in the sail, and Vetch finished his sleep, though uneasily, in the stern of the boat. At noon they ate. Ged doled their food out sparingly, and the portent of this was plain, but both of them chewed their bit of salt fish and wheaten cake, and neither said anything.

All afternoon they cleaved eastward never turning nor slackening pace. Once Ged broke his silence, saying, "Do you hold with those who think the world is all landless sea beyond the Outer Reaches, or with those who imagine other Archipelagoes or vast undiscovered lands on the other face of the world?"

"At this time," said Vetch, "I hold with those who think the world has but one face, and he who sails too far will fall off the edge of it."

Ged did not smile; there was no mirth left in him. "Who knows what a man might meet, out there? Not we, who keep always to our coasts and shores."

"Some have sought to know, and have not returned. And no ship has ever come to us from lands we do not know."

Ged made no reply.

All that day, all that night they went driven by the powerful wind of magery over the great swells of ocean, eastward. Ged kept watch from dusk till dawn, for in darkness the force that drew or drove him grew stronger yet. Always he watched ahead, though his eyes in the moonless night could see no more than the painted eyes aside the boat's blind prow. By daybreak his dark face was grey with weariness, and he was so cramped with cold that he could hardly stretch out to rest. He said whispering, "Hold the magewind from the west, Estarriol," and then he slept.

There was no sunrise, and presently rain came beating across the bow from the northeast. It was no storm, only the long, cold winds and rains of winter. Soon all things in the open boat were wet through, despite the sailcloth cover they had bought; and Vetch felt as if he too were soaked clear to the bone; and Ged shivered in his sleep. In pity for his friend, and perhaps for himself, Vetch tried to turn aside for a little that rude ceaseless wind that bore the rain. But though, following Ged's will, he could keep the magewind strong and steady, his weatherworking had small power here so far from land, and the wind of the Open Sea did not listen to his voice.

And at this a certain fear came into Vetch, as he began to wonder how much wizardly power would be left to him and Ged, if they went on and on away from the lands where men were meant to live.

Ged watched again that night, and all night held the boat eastward. When day came the world's wind slackened somewhat, and the sun shone fitfully; but the great swells ran so high that *Lookfar* must tilt and climb up them as if they were hills, and hang at the hillcrest and plunge suddenly, and climb up the next again, and the next, and the next, unending.

In the evening of that day Vetch spoke out of long silence. "My friend," he said, "you spoke once as if sure we would come to land at last. I would not question your vision but for this, that it might be a trick, a deception made by that which you follow, to lure you on farther than a man can go over ocean. For our power may change and weaken on strange seas. And a shadow does not tire, or starve, or drown."

They sat side by side on the thwart, yet Ged looked at him now as if from a distance, across a wide abyss. His eyes were troubled, and he was slow to answer.

At last he said, "Estarriol, we are coming near."

Hearing his words, his friend knew them to be true. He was afraid, then. But he put his hand on Ged's shoulder and said only, "Well, then, good, that is good."

Again that night Ged watched, for he could not sleep in the dark. Nor would he sleep when the third day came. Still they ran with that ceaseless, light, terrible swiftness over the sea, and Vetch wondered at Ged's power that could hold so strong a magewind hour after hour, here on the Open Sea where Vetch felt his own power all weakened and astray. And they went on, until it seemed to Vetch that what Ged had spoken would come true, and they were going beyond the sources of the sea and eastward behind the gates of daylight. Ged stayed forward in the boat, looking ahead as always. But he was not watching the ocean now, or not the ocean that Vetch saw, a waste of heaving water to the rim of the sky. In Ged's eyes there was a dark vision that overlapped and veiled the grey sea and the grey sky, and the darkness grew, and the veil thickened. None of this was visible to Vetch, except when he looked at his friend's face; then he too saw the darkness for a moment. They went on, and on. And it was as if, though one wind drove them in one boat, Vetch went east over the world's sea, while Ged went alone into a realm where there was no east or west, no rising or setting of the sun, or of the stars.

Ged stood up suddenly in the prow, and spoke aloud. The magewind dropped. *Lookfar* lost headway, and rose and fell on the vast surges like a chip of wood. Though the world's wind blew strong as ever straight from the north now, the brown sail hung slack, unstirred. And so the boat hung on the waves, swung by their great slow swinging, but going no direction.

Ged said, "Take down the sail," and Vetch did so quickly, while Ged unlashed the oars and set them in the locks and bent his back to rowing.

Vetch, seeing only the waves heaving up and down clear to the end of sight, could not understand why they went now by oars; but he waited, and presently he was aware that the world's wind was growing faint and the swells diminishing. The climb and plunge of the boat grew less and less, till at last she seemed to go forward under Ged's strong oarstrokes over water that lay almost still, as in a land-locked bay. And though Vetch could not see what Ged saw, when between his strokes he looked ever and again over his shoulder at what lay before the boat's way— though Vetch could not see the dark slopes beneath unmoving stars, yet he began to see with his wizard's eye a darkness that welled up in the hollows of the waves all around the boat, and he saw the billows grow low and sluggish as they were choked with sand.

If this were an enchantment of illusion, it was powerful beyond belief; to make the Open Sea seem land. Trying to collect his wits and courage, Vetch spoke the Revelation-spell, watching between each slow-syllabled word for change or tremor of illusion in this strange drying and shallowing of the abyss of ocean. But there was none. Perhaps the spell, though it should affect only his own vision and not the magic at work about them, had no power here. Or perhaps there was no illusion, and they had come to world's end.

Unheeding, Ged rowed always slower, looking over his shoulder, choosing a way among channels or shoals and shallows that he alone could see. The boat shuddered as her keel dragged. Under that keel lay the vast deeps of the sea, yet they were aground. Ged drew the oars up rattling in their locks, and that noise was terrible, for there was no other sound. All sounds of water, wind, wood, sail, were gone, lost in a huge profound silence that might have been unbroken for ever. The boat lay motionless. No breath of wind moved. The sea had turned to sand, shadowy, unstirred. Nothing moved in the dark sky or on that dry unreal ground that went on and on into gathering darkness all around the boat as far as eye could see.

Ged stood up, and took his staff, and lightly stepped over the side of the boat. Vetch thought to see him fall and sink down in the sea, the sea that surely was there behind this dry, dim veil that hid away water, sky, and light. But there was no sea any more. Ged walked away from the boat. The dark sand showed his footprints where he went, and whispered a little under his step.

His staff began to shine, not with the werelight but with a clear white glow, that soon grew so bright that it reddened his fingers where they held the radiant wood.

He strode forward, away from the boat, but in no direction. There were no directions here, no north or south or east or west, only towards and away.

To Vetch, watching, the light he bore seemed like a great slow star that moved through the darkness. And the darkness about it thickened, blackened, drew together. This also Ged saw, watching always ahead through the light. And after a while he saw at the faint outermost edge of the light a shadow that came towards him over the sand.

At first it was shapeless, but as it drew nearer it took on the look of a man. An old man it seemed, grey and grim, coming towards Ged; but even as Ged saw his father the smith in that figure, he saw that it was not an old man but a young one. It was Jasper: Jasper's insolent handsome young face, and silver-clasped grey cloak, and stiff stride. Hateful was the look he fixed on Ged across the dark intervening air. Ged did not stop, but slowed his pace, and as he went forward he raised his staff up a little higher. It brightened, and in its light the look of Jasper fell from the figure that approached, and it became Pechvarry. But Pechvarry's face was all bloated and pallid like the face of a drowned man, and he reached out his hand strangely as if beckoning. Still Ged did not stop, but went forward, though there were only a few yards left between them now. Then the thing that faced him changed utterly, spreading out to either side as if it opened enormous thin wings, and it writhed, and swelled, and shrank again. Ged saw in it for an instant Skiorh's white face, and then a pair of clouded, staring eyes, and then suddenly a fearful face he did not know, man or monster, with writhing lips and eyes that were like pits going back into black emptiness.

At that Ged lifted up the staff high, and the radiance of it brightened intolerably, burning with so white and great a light that it compelled and harrowed even that ancient darkness. In that light all form of man sloughed off the thing that came towards

Ged. It drew together and shrank and blackened, crawling on four short taloned legs upon the sand. But still it came forward, lifting up to him a blind unformed snout without lips or ears or eyes. As they came right together it became utterly black in the white mage-radiance that burned about it, and it heaved itself upright. In silence, man and shadow met face to face, and stopped.

Aloud and clearly, breaking that old silence, Ged spoke the shadow's name and in the same moment the shadow spoke without lips or tongue, saying the same word: "Ged." And the two voices were one voice.

Ged reached out his hands, dropping his staff, and took hold of his shadow, of the black self that reached out to him. Light and darkness met, and joined, and were one.

But to Vetch, watching in terror through the dark twilight from far off over the sand, it seemed that Ged was overcome, for he saw the clear radiance fail and grow dim. Rage and despair filled him, and he sprang out on the sand to help his friend or die with him, and ran towards that small fading glimmer of light in the empty dusk of the dry land. But as he ran the sand sank under his feet, and he struggled in it as in quicksand, as through a heavy flow of water: until with a roar of noise and a glory of daylight, and the bitter cold of winter, and the bitter taste of salt, the world was restored to him and he floundered in the sudden, true, and living sea.

Nearby the boat rocked on the grey waves, empty. Vetch could see nothing else on the water; the battering wave-tops filled his eyes and blinded him. No strong swimmer, he struggled as best he could to the boat, and pulled himself up into her. Coughing and trying to wipe away the water that streamed from his hair, he looked about desperately, not knowing now which way to look. And at last he made out something dark among the waves, a long way off across what had been sand and now was wild water. Then he leapt to the oars and rowed mightily to his friend, and catching Ged's arms helped and hauled him up over the side.

Ged was dazed and his eyes stared as if they saw nothing, but there was no hurt to be seen on him. His staff, black yew wood, all radiance quenched, was grasped in his right hand, and he would not let go of it. He said no word. Spent and soaked and shaking he lay huddled up against the mast, never looking at Vetch who raised the sail and turned the boat to catch the north-east wind. He saw nothing of the world until, straight ahead of their course, in the sky that darkened where the sun had set, between long clouds in a bay of clear blue light, the new moon shone: a ring of ivory, a rim of horn, reflected sunlight shining across the ocean of the dark.

Ged lifted his face and gazed at that remote bright crescent in the west.

He gazed for a long time, and then he stood up erect, holding his staff in his two hands as a warrior holds his long sword. He looked about at the sky, the sea, the brown swelling sail above him, his friend's face.

"Estarriol," he said, "look, it is done. It is over." He laughed. "The wound is healed," he said, "I am whole, I am free." Then he bent over and hid his face in his arms, weeping like a boy.

Until that moment Vetch had watched him with an anxious dread, for he was not sure what had happened there in the dark land. He did not know if this was Ged in the boat with him, and his hand had been for hours ready to the anchor, to stave in the boat's planking and sink her there in midsea, rather than carry back to the harbors of Earthsea the evil thing that he feared might have taken Ged's look and form. Now when he saw his friend and heard him speak, his doubt vanished. And he began to see the truth, that Ged had neither lost nor won but, naming the shadow of his death with his own name, had made himself whole: a man: who, knowing his whole true self, cannot be used or possessed by any power other than himself, and whose life therefore is lived for life's sake and never in the service of ruin, or pain, or hatred, or the dark. In the *Creation of Éa*, which is the oldest song, it is said, "Only in silence the word, only in dark the light, only in dying life: bright the hawk's flight on the empty sky." That song Vetch sang aloud now as he held the boat westward, going before the cold wind of the winter night that blew at their backs from the vastness of the Open Sea.

Eight days they sailed and eight again, before they came in sight of land. Many times they had to refill their waterskin with spell-sweetened water of the sea; and they fished, but even when they called out fisher-man's charms they caught very little, for the fish of the Open Sea do not know their own names and pay no heed to magic. When they had nothing left to eat but a few scraps of smoked meat Ged remembered what Yarrow had said when he stole the cake from the hearth, that he would regret his theft when he came to hunger on the sea; but hungry as he was the remembrance pleased him. For she had also said that he, with her brother, would come home again.

The magewind had borne them for only three days eastward, yet sixteen days they sailed westward to re-turn. No men have ever returned from so far out on the Open Sea as did the young wizards Estarriol and Ged in the Fallows of winter in their open fishing-boat. They met no great storms, and steered steadily enough by the compass and by the star Tolbegren, taking a course somewhat northward of their out-bound way. Thus they did not come back to Asto-well, but passing by Far Toly and Sneg without sight-ing them, first raised land off the southernmost cape of Koppish. Over the waves they saw cliffs of stone rise like a great fortress. Seabirds cried wheeling over the breakers, and smoke of the hearthfires of small villages drifted blue on the wind.

From there the voyage to Iffish was not long. They came in to Ismay harbor on a still, dark evening before snow. They tied up the boat *Lookfar* that had borne them to the coasts of death's kingdom and back, and went up through the narrow streets to the wizard's house. Their hearts were very light as they entered into the firelight and warmth under that roof; and Yarrow ran to meet them, crying with joy.

If Estarriol of Iffish kept his promise and made a
song of that first great deed of Ged's, it has been lost.
There is a tale told in the East Reach of a boat that
ran aground, days out from any shore, over the abyss
of ocean. In Iffish they say it was Estarriol who sailed
that boat, but in Tok they say it was two fishermen
blown by a storm far out on the Open Sea, and in
Holp the tale is of a Holpish fisherman, and tells that
he could not move his boat from the unseen sands it
grounded on, and so wanders there yet. So of the
song of the Shadow there remain only a few scraps of
legend, carried like driftwood from isle to isle over
the long years. But in the *Deed of Ged* nothing is
told of that voyage nor of Ged's meeting with the
shadow, before ever he sailed the Dragon's Run unscathed, or brought back the Ring of Erreth-Akbe
from the Tombs of Atuan to Havnor, or came at last
to Roke once more, as Archmage of all the islands of
the world.

# ABOUT THE AUTHOR

URSULA KROEBER LE GUIN was born in Berkeley, California, in 1929, daughter of the anthropologist Alfred L. Kroeber and the writer Theodora Kroeber, author of *Ishi in Two Worlds* and other books. She attended Radcliffe College and Columbia University, and during a Fulbright year in Paris married a young historian, Charles Le Guin. Mrs. Le Guin's published works include poetry, stories and several science fiction novels: *Rocannon's World, Planet of Exile, City of Illusions, The Lathe of Heaven* and *The Left Hand of Darkness,* which was awarded the Hugo and Nebula awards for best science fiction novel for 1969. *A Wizard of Earthsea,* the first book in Mrs. Le Guin's Earthsea trilogy, was awarded the Boston *Globe* Horn Book Award for Excellence in 1969, and was followed by *The Tombs of Atuan,* which won the Newbery Award, and *The Farthest Shore,* which was the National Book Award-winner for Children's Books in 1973. Mrs. Le Guin's most recent novel, *The Dispossessed,* was the 1974 Nebula Award-winner. Ursula K. Le Guin currently lives in Portland, Oregon, with her husband, two daughters (Elisabeth and Caroline) and one son (Theodore).

# ABOUT THE ILLUSTRATOR

RUTH ROBBINS illustrated *A Penny and a Perriwinkle, Fisherman's Luck, Wild Animals of the Far West, Stories California Indians Told* and *Ishi, Last of His Tribe* (an ALA Notable Book). She is the author of *Baboushka and the Three Kings* (Caldecott Award), *The Emperor and the Drummer Boy* (an ALA Notable Book) and *Harlequin and Mother Goose.* She lives in Berkeley, California, with her husband and son.